HUNTING PARTY

HUNTING PARTY

a novel

Agnès Desarthe

Translated by Christiana Hills

Introduction by Jessie Chaffee

The Unnamed Press
Los Angeles, CA

The Unnamed Press
P.O. Box 411272
Los Angeles, CA 90041
Published in North America by The Unnamed Press.
1 3 5 7 9 10 8 6 4 2
Copyright 2012 © Editions de l'Olivier

Translation Copyright 2018 © Christiana Hills
Foreword Copyright 2018 © Jessie Chaffee

ISBN: 978-1944700-7-13

Library of Congress Control Number: 2018931446

Originally published in the French as *Une partie de chasse* by Editions de l'Olivier.

Distributed by Publishers Group West

Designed & typeset by Jaya Nicely

**This work received the French Voices Award
for excellence in publication and translation.
French Voices is a program created and funded
by the French Embassy in the United States and
FACE (French American Cultural Exchange).**

Table of Contents

Introduction

The Beautiful Brutality of Existence

"A black tunnel opens up before his eyes. He doesn't know how deep it is, he can't see the bottom."

In one of the key moments in *Hunting Party*, the protagonist, Tristan, finds himself burrowing into the earth, into a void of his own making, while a storm rages around him. This scene, terrifying and euphoric, is not unlike the experience of reading Agnès Desarthe, who immerses us in the simultaneous beauty and violence of nature, language, and love. Part philosophical meditation and part thrilling adventure, this novel—her fifth to be published in English translation—reads like a myth, and Desarthe operates on that expansive scale. With inventiveness and daring, she produces talking animals, biblical floods, the end of the world, while also delving in to examine the smallest exchanges of intimacy between people and within oneself. Throughout she brings the reader to the same point of reckoning as she does her protagonist—suspended over the abyss, trying to decipher precisely what is gazing back at us.

Tristan has joined the local hunting party of three men at the urging of his wife, Emma, in an effort to better "fit into" the small French village where the couple has settled. We quickly learn that at stake is not only the couple's assimilation but also the survival of their marriage. More prone to reflection than violence, Tristan has seemingly little in common with his peers, who relish the thrill of ending life. But moments into the hunt, it is Tristan who takes the first shot, injuring a small rabbit to whom he becomes inextricably bound. When one of the hunters is swallowed up by a literal void—a hole in the ground—Tristan follows him, dying rabbit in tow, and as the afternoon devolves into chaos both natural and man-made, the rabbit engages him in a spirited dialogue about free will, mortality, and desire.

Desarthe challenges the confines of genre with the same deftness that she dissolves the boundaries between the interior worlds of her characters and their exterior landscapes, until they become one and the same. Descending into the earth, Tristan feels that "inside him, like outside, a storm is brewing," and "the more his hands feel the earth, the more they're learning about the nature of what's going to sweep over them." The theme of interior and exterior states repeats as Tristan confronts the ghosts of his past, the fragility of this present, and the "persistent pain of exile" that he feels, a pain that poses a question pertinent to all the book's characters, not to mention its readers: Can we ever truly know another person? Can we ever know ourselves? And, as Tristan wonders, "where can this missing link be found—inside or outside of himself?"

Knowing and being known are, in part, an issue of translation. Tristan reflects on his time as a student in England, where he struggled to decode an unfamiliar culture and to comprehend a new language, an experience that made him feel as much of an outsider as he does on the ill-fated hunt. But though Desarthe questions the limitations of language, she also conveys its limitless joys as Tristan begins to master English: "His voice changes, the muscles in his cheeks and lips reorganize themselves around this new nucleus . . . He's being reborn." One of the pleasures of reading *Hunting Party* is Desarthe's own use of language, beautifully translated by Christiana Hills. When Tristan recounts his final days with his ill mother, he describes the way her massless body allowed light to filter through, like "a strainer, a wire fence, a cheesecloth." Desarthe's prose, in Hills's translation, has a similar translucent quality. The story is dense with meaning, but the language is airy, allowing the ideas to filter through, just as the light does in the warren in which Tristan finds himself, the sun "leaping to and fro . . . as precise as a lacemaker's needle."

Though *Hunting Party* feels in many ways outside of time, the questions it poses about masculinity, violence, and the relationship between them are extremely timely. The narrative is permeated with overt and underlying violence, Chekhov's gun looming large as both metaphor and reality. Tristan wonders at the story's beginning "how an argument ends when you have a loaded gun in your hands." Emma is an aspiring author, and her books are filled with bodies that have been brutalized and burned, because, she explains to her husband, violence in ever-increasing amounts is the only way to keep people's attention in a culture that has grown inured to it. In Desarthe's world, one of the things gazing back from the abyss is this endless propensity for violence. "The last refuge of creativity lies in destruction," Emma says. "Art has to plant a bomb."

In such a context, what happens to a gentle, deeply feeling man who is "at home in solitude," who "dreads the fight. The loaded guns. The restless bullets"? Where does he fit? The answer—and the problem—of course, is that he doesn't fit, because there isn't room in narrow definitions of masculinity for a man like Tristan. As his mother asks him in childhood, "Do boys like you even exist?" Not nearly enough of them. And as Tristan clumsily mimics the gait and callousness of his companions, one of the central threats is that he may be found out for precisely what he is not.

The philosophical rabbit is likewise an outsider in his species. In the book's opening, he wishes for a longer life than the one nature dictates for him. What he desires is not only the pleasures that such an extended existence would bring, but also the pains that inevitably accompany them: the "magnificent, speechless sorrow" of moving from childhood into adulthood; the wisdom of old age and its weariness; and, above all, love, along with "the infinite luxury of losing it." Violence may dominate the narrative, but it is love that comes into sharp focus as a force that brings with it the same ecstasy and destruction as the storm that sweeps through the valley, a force that creates the void but also serves as its antidote. And if, as Tristan's mother teaches him, violence is "written in our DNA," so too, Desarthe seems to suggest, is our capacity for love.

Hunting Party is about nothing less than the search for meaning—in the world, within oneself, and, most vitally, in relation to others. In disappearing into the abyss of his past and his present, Tristan contends with the vulnerability of love, the inevitability of loss, and the beauty to be found in both. "What is this solemn thing that hurts, that takes the heart like a bear claw and crushes it?" he wonders as he is falling in love with Emma. "His jaw tightened against a sob born from his gratitude, from his fear of losing her," for "the finiteness of others. That's where love is born." It is in this vulnerability that Desarthe offers a new kind of hero, in a moment when it is sorely needed. Emma sends her husband out with a gun to prove that he is a man, but in Desarthe's story, the hero doesn't wield a gun. Rather the hero is the person most willing to be vulnerable, the person most willing to burrow into the possibility of loss. The hero is a lover.

—Jessie Chaffee, author of *Florence in Ecstasy*

HUNTING PARTY

1

I'd love to die of natural causes. I'd like to grow old. None of my kind grows old. We depart in the prime of our lives.

I'd love to have time to leave childhood, to know the poignant nostalgia that grips teenagers' hearts. Something in them mourns the child they no longer are, and it's a magnificent, speechless sorrow.

I'd like to get bored, to know disgust. Then, to enjoy the relief that comes with maturity.

I'd like to have the time to know love and the infinite luxury of losing it.

"I don't love you anymore, it's over; we've been seeing each other for too long, I don't feel anything for you now."

Often, in order to hurt myself, to fully feel the cruelty of my fate, I play out this impossible scene in my head, I repeat to myself this line that I will never say out loud.

I have a big imagination. They say it's rare in our family line. My mother told me so. She thought I was smarter than the others. She used to say she didn't entirely understand me. She would tilt her head while uttering these words, and the sun, held captive for a moment in her iris, would pierce my retina.

She died, of course. Very quickly. She hardly said much to me. None of us has time for anything, those who are left. But she told me this anyway, that I have a big imagination, and probably a larger brain than my brothers, my cousins, my ancestors, so I use it. I pretend to be old.

"Old," "aged," "elderly"—these words make me tremble with pain and joy. They're the loveliest, sweetest, and most dreadful words of our language. I dare to utter them. I know the risk I take. My heart could give way from an excess of delight. But I bet on the excellence of my heart, I don't have a choice. I bet on the caliber of each one of my organs and muscles. I am made to last, to endure, to survive. I'm going to make it. I might be the only one, but who knows? Once I'm seasoned and worn out, when my teeth are missing and my blood flows less swiftly through my veins, I'll be able to teach others, take a few young ones under my wing and tell them my secrets, my tricks, explain to them that it's possible. "Look at me! See my ears, weary and drooping, my lazy eyelid that half covers my right eye. The hump on my back. My tired whiskers."

I will be their prophet; I will find a territory; I will organize the resistance. Too long have we suffered, too long have we given in to our fate.

We don't have memories. We don't have time to build up remembrances, experiences. With each birth, the entire species starts all over again, and we run, we jump, panicked, in zigzags. No sooner have we felt the sun on our brows, the warmth of a mother's milk in our throats, than we must leave home, set off, catch up with the lateness that's been written in our genetic code since the beginning of time. Late, late, we're always too late. The threat is inscribed in each one of us. The threat is our destiny.

For the moment, I am alone. I've found a place. I'm holding on. I must somehow manage to think, to wait, to get myself organized. It's unnatural. My tendons are itching to go. My instinct dictates flight, but I've seen too many who, in fleeing, were caught, killed in motion.

I attempt stillness; I attempt calm. But my whole body yearns to escape, to slip away. I must control it, impose a law on it that I'll make up as I go along. I must be my own tyrant.

In order to give myself courage, I repeat my motto, "To die of natural causes, to die of old age." Ah! To be worthy of one's own demise, to ultimately wish for it, to experience weariness.

Soon, I will have to go out, find something to eat.

Soon, I will have to find myself a companion.

I'll know how to screw her like I'm supposed to. No need to think about it. It's inscribed in us. But that's the trap: doing what you know how to do. That's what we die from, from our bodies' tyranny and our lack of foresight.

I'll be abstinent. As soon as the desire arises, I'll repress it. Dying of hunger, is that a natural death? Dying of loneliness, of grief?

No.

There must be another way. I'm having a hard time concentrating, because of hunger, because of urgency, because of my petrified limbs begging for action, for speed. It's like an impulse within me, a force that disregards my being, despises my willpower. The same force that transforms a stem into a trunk, that makes thunder strike, waves crash and break, volcanoes erupt, planets follow their orbits in the heavens. My body is too small for it; I feel torn apart. This force will rip me open if I try to subdue it. I'm still holding on, but this tingling under my skin tells me I'm not going to last much longer. I'm going to give in, like elastic, a catapult, a bow, and burst out like a cannonball, a lead bullet.

The bullet shoots from the rifle the instant I shoot out of my hole. What a beautiful encounter. An encounter in time, in the synchronic perfection of chance. The hunter didn't do it deliberately. He couldn't have known that my paws would propel me out of the earth at that very second. He didn't see me. He didn't aim, but I'm lying here stunned, awestruck, admiring the beauty of the unexpected, admiring the inevitable. I'm so young and I'm going to die. It's impossible. I had such a big, bright future in store. I couldn't have inherited this awareness for nothing. Someone, somewhere, must have had an idea in the back of their mind. Or maybe not.

I'm so small; I'm so sweet. What a shame. The man who picks me up looks like me. We stare at each other. His thumb is on my heart, which is still beating. He's crying. He tries to hide. He doesn't want anyone to see him. He's probably not alone. I hear a voice a little farther away. A man's voice.

2

"What the fuck are you doing? You didn't shoot yourself in the foot, did you?"

Bursts of raucous laughter.

A young man, with shaky knees, holds a cottontail rabbit in his right hand. Dawn is breaking. A pearly vapor is foaming up at the top of the meadow. With a thumb on the animal's heart, the man feels the rapid heartbeats, which excite his own cardiac rhythm. He is crying. He has never killed anything or anyone. But the rabbit isn't dead. If the heart is beating, it means he's alive. Don't show him to the others. Keep him. Look after him. Care for him.

Here come the dogs.

He doesn't like dogs. He's always been afraid of them. They're going to smell the rabbit. They're trained for it. They're going to betray him, and then Dumestre's big hands, *crack*, a quarter turn will suffice. The head will hang down, as though it's lost interest in the body, in a blasé pose that makes death appear like a welcome nap, a dreamless, pleasureless sleep.

The young man opens his gamebag, a lovely name, a practical object, simple, which keeps its promises—it was Dumestre who let him borrow it—and slips the trembling rabbit under the dish towel he took when he left the house. He does that. All the time. A sort of compulsive habit. Leaving with a dish towel. At restaurants, he sometimes takes the cloth napkin with him. The dish towel smells like oranges; it came from the fruit bowl. Maybe the dogs will be put off by the scent.

He can still hear the shot's echo in the air, as though the atmosphere refused to accept the intrusion. No wind in the trees to dissolve it; no breeze in the grass to carry it away. Something has been paralyzed, petrified.

"Aren't you going to say something? You hurt or what? You're not dead, are you?"

Raucous bursts of laughter once more. Closer. And *wham!* A big slap on the back nearly knocks him over. The young man smiles.

"Sorry," he says.

"It's okay, you didn't wake anybody up. We're not sleeping!" The laughter continues.

Three men surround him. Dumestre: a barrel mounted on two stiff legs, neck of a bull, large, flat head, crimson face from which his eyes emerge, slightly bulging, like two snails. Farnèse: stealthy, pale blue eyes matching his gray complexion, a spectacular thinness, an alcoholic thinness. Peretti: broad hips, hollow chest, bowed legs, weak jawline that merges with his throat, eyes both intelligent and fearful, mouth of a guilty little boy.

Three men. He is the fourth. It's a hunting party. Joking, beer, warm blood, the scent of dogs, leather, steel, wood.

Tristan brings his hand up to his face, breathes in. The orange fragrance from the dish towel is trapped in his palm. It calms his racing heart.

"Would ya look at that, the dogs are making a fuss over you. Incredible! A success like that with the mutts. You're the animals' friend, am I right?"

Yes, thinks Tristan, who feels the rabbit's heart beating too slowly, too dully against his hipbone.

Live, he silently orders the rabbit. If you live, then everything is possible. What went wrong will be made right.

The three hunters surround him. Farnèse gives him a friendly punch in the shoulder. Peretti deals a light smack to the back of his skull. Dumestre stares at him.

"Did you see something? Why'd you shoot?"

"The shot went off on its own," says Tristan.

The three others have a good laugh.

"Premature ejaculation?" Dumestre asks.

Farnèse and Peretti laugh louder than ever.

Tristan laughs with them.

3

Hunting was Emma's idea. A good way to fit in, she had said to him. We'll never make it if you don't fit in. The men around here have certain habits, pleasures you must share. The women will reject me, no matter what I do. But you, you have a chance. You could make it. Do it for us both. Do it for me. I can't live alone. Even alone with you. Our love will die of it. We need other people. *I* need them. For us, so that you can go on loving me.

Tristan knows that if he were now brandishing the moribund rabbit, he would've won.

Beginner's luck, the other three would laugh, but they'd grant him respect. Tristan would fit in and Emma would be reassured.

"In another time, I could've gone to church on Sundays," she says. "That would have been enough. But no one goes anymore. So..."

"So fine, I'll go hunting with them."

"You'll see, it's nothing, it's easy."

"Easy to kill an innocent animal?"

"You won't have to kill anything. You'll go along with them, that's all. You imitate them, you speak like them. You laugh at their jokes. You congratulate them. You ask their advice. They'll take you under their wing."

"They'll treat me like a queer."

"No! They don't even know what that is. Trust me, my love. Go on. Straighten your shoulders. There. Make your manly face."

He furrows his brow.

She bursts out laughing.

"Even *you* don't believe it."

"Yes, I do. I could eat you up..."

She kisses him. The scent rising from between her breasts, at once piercing and dull, intoxicates Tristan, hardens him, thrills him.

"Okay, fine, you win. I'll go on Sunday."

"Not to Mass, to the hunt. Hunting," she says, "will always exist."

4

Emma is taller than he is. Heavier as well. She looks like an Indian chief, he says to himself sometimes. He adores her body. It's his domain. The only territory where he's ever felt at home. He has become its cartographer, its expert.

"What are you doing?" she asks.

"I'm looking at you."

"Again?"

He nods.

5

Tristan doesn't take the rabbit out of the gamebag. He waits for the dogs to calm down, pick up another scent. A hen pheasant flutters out of a thicket. It slowly moves forward, in a cautious, stupid way. Farnèse takes aim, his finger quivering on the trigger. He shoots.

"Shit, Farnèse!" Dumestre shouts. "You busted its head open. Talk about carnage!"

The bird runs around, decapitated, for a yard or two, a fountain of blood on two legs.

Tristan suppresses the urge to vomit. He slips his hand into his bag. With the tips of his fingers, he strokes the rabbit's back, feels a tiny vibration under the pad of his middle finger. Don't die, he thinks.

I'm not dying, answers the mute rabbit. I'm persevering. I'm starting a new life, a surplus. I see our encounter as a miracle. I don't know how you did it, you clumsy young man, friend to animals, but you didn't touch a single vital organ. The proof: I'm thinking. I'm persevering. I'm focusing on healing as quickly as possible. I promise

not to lose any blood. I'm commanding my veins to preserve their wholeness. The bullet only grazed my muzzle.
I was knocked out. I'm swallowing the trickle of scarlet
saliva staining my chops. You are my chance of a lifetime.
I'm not hungry anymore. You've freed me from any sense
of urgency. Now I've been removed from my destiny.
Young man, you're full of kindness. I adore you.

The dogs sniff the pheasant's remains. They growl; they
yap. Farnèse stares at the ground between his feet. He's
ashamed. Tristan doesn't understand why.

"Good shot, in any case," he ventures.

"This kid's funny," says Dumestre. "You're funny," he
repeats for Tristan. "That's some sense of humor, huh? I
love humor, but it's not easy. You have to work at it."

Tristan nods in agreement. He's not sure whether he's
passed the test. He's labeled "the joker." That's not what
Emma had in mind. She was thinking Ulysses, she was
thinking Jason, Achilles, even. What trophy will he be carrying when he crosses the doorstep of their house?

"Anyone want some coffee?"

Peretti's treat. He brought a thermos. The four of them
use the same cup. The coffee is very strong and very sweet.
It has an iron aftertaste.

"That hits the spot," says Tristan.

"It's hot, that's why," says Peretti.

"It's 'cause we're here," says Dumestre. "Everything
you eat in the forest, everything you drink in the forest, is

better. It's the air. Especially in the morning, like now. The leaves sweat during the night. When you breathe, the air that goes into your lungs is different. It's filled with the leaves' sweat. The coffee is different too."

"That's all in your head," says Farnèse.

"You're a dick," says Dumestre.

"No, *you're* the dick."

Tristan wonders how an argument ends when you have a loaded gun in your hands.

6

"You're sure the woman has to be cut open before being burned alive?"

"Yes. Why? Don't you like it?"

Tristan sets the warm pages on the kitchen table as they come out of the printer. Emma stares at him, a look of defiance in her eyes.

"That's how it is now," she explains. "You have to say everything. Stretch the limits. People are numb. They have to be shocked, woken up. We've seen everything, heard everything. Blasé—know the word? That's what we are. Blasé. Take the most inventive geniuses of our time, you know where they are? In prisons and psychiatric wards. They're serial killers who've used mathematical models, philosophical models. We've worked so hard to prolong our lives, to improve them, that the last refuge of creativity lies in destruction. Art has to plant a bomb. If you don't plant a bomb, you're dead."

Tristan can't think of a response. Emma is always right. And he's always trailing a little behind, as if he doesn't want to see things as they really are. She writes novels. But no one's heard of her. They don't talk about her in the newspapers. Her photo isn't published anywhere. In the village, people think she knits, because of the scarves, long and heavy like boa constrictors, that Tristan wears around his neck.

When he met her, he didn't know she was a writer. She was working as a waitress at a pub in southeast London where he sometimes went to have a Sprite after class.

"French?" she had asked him one evening, even though he hadn't said a word.

"How'd you know?"

"It's obvious."

"And you?"

"Me too. Isn't it obvious?"

Laughing, she went back to the bar without taking his order. She jabbered something in English to the manager—bald with glasses, pocket Bible in hand, standing straight as a totem pole behind the counter—and brought Tristan a beer.

He had never drunk anything like it. But then again, was this even a drink? It was heavy in his mouth, thick, slightly viscous, like porridge.

"You have to adapt, kid," she said, straddling a chair she'd turned around to face him, like at the cabaret, he thought. "You have to fit in. Sprite, that's American crap. In Marseille, you drink pastis; in Paris, coffee; in London, it's Guinness. Get it? And not timid little swallows like a granny sipping her tea. You knock it back, and afterward you lick the froth off your lips. What brings you here?"

"I come after class."

"What're you studying?"

"Russian Symbolist poetry."

"To do what?"

"I don't know. When I was a kid, my mom took me to the Opéra Garnier one evening. It was *Eugene Onegin*. '*Tebya lyublyu Tatyanu*'—I remember the words."

"Pushkin wasn't a Symbolist."

"No."

How did she know that? he wondered. Who's interested in Russian poetry? Even he wasn't that passionate about it. He had been sent to London to study and, when the time came to choose his classes, he had remembered that evening with his mother. The tears on her face. He had often seen her cry, in despair, in rage, in drunkenness, in turmoil. That time, it was something else. He hadn't understood what, but he had felt infinitely relieved.

He didn't get the chance to ask the waitress what she knew about Russians and the rest. She'd jumped up to serve other customers.

Sometime later, she had confessed: "I was so ashamed."

"Ashamed of what?"

"Of my way of doing things. Approaching you, completely hysterical. Like a bull in a china shop. I have a hard time controlling my emotions. That's the problem incredibly shy people have. I'm not talking about you. You're not shy. You're lots of things, but you're not shy. But I'm really shy. So, when I make a move, I overdo it, all hell breaks loose. I'm ridiculous."

"It's true."

"Bastard."

"I'm being honest," he declared, sounding both knowledgeable and ironic.

"You're a misfit. That's what I'd say. A total misfit."

They were sitting on a bench in Brockwell Park that was dedicated to the memory of Linda B. Delaweare by her loving husband.

"Misfit," she repeated.

Then she leaned toward him, abruptly, like the incredibly shy person she was, and kissed him for the first time. Tristan was floored. If someone had cut open his stomach, he couldn't have been more surprised or more touched. There was so much vulnerability in that gesture, so much awkwardness. The desperation of her lips. She kissed like an ugly girl, as if she were apologizing.

"You're the most beautiful woman I've ever seen," he told her, caressing her temples, her forehead.

"In the end, I actually do appreciate your honesty."

The wind picked up at that moment, hurling a huge purple cloud down to the level of the lush grass, which was bent over by the storm. The hail fell, a shower of transparent pebbles beating down on the paths' warm asphalt, imitating a stampede of a thousand tiny horses.

They ran to the garden flat where Emma lived, without holding hands, without touching each other, saving their own skins, terrified by the power of the air pressing down on their backs, the violence of the diamonds being fired down from the sky, and the certainty that they had found each other, that this was for life, forever, true love, the real deal, even though they were still so young. What a waste!

they thought. What a waste! Cast down by the weight of their destiny, the new, eternal responsibility, the frightening solemnity of their passion.

7

"We're not taking it?" asks Tristan, pointing to the decapitated hen the dogs were attacking.

"No," replies Dumestre. "It'll get shit all over everything. Apologize, Farnèse."

"Why should I apologize?" retorts Farnèse, chin thrust out, rifle pointed at Dumestre.

"Say sorry to the hen."

Peretti laughs softly. He says, "Come on," in a voice so low that no one hears him.

"It's my fault," Tristan asserts, trying to interfere.

The sun, which has just risen above the horizon, poses a golden accusative finger on Farnèse's face. He squints.

"Sorry, hen," he mumbles, the barrel of his gun pointed toward the ground. And then, after a moment, "Sorry, Mother Nature. Sorry, Diana the huntress, goddess of the forest. Sorry—"

"That's enough," says Dumestre. "Stop your nonsense. You fire like a barbarian, you say sorry. That's all. We're not pigs. We're not criminals. There are rules. We're not monsters. We're not maniacs."

"We're nice guys," Peretti concludes, his smile glued on his face.

Tristan feels like something has gone amiss in his initiation. He had dreaded killing, but the spectacle he's watching now is more complicated than death.

"What do we do now?" he asks.

"We keep going," Dumestre answers.

They all follow him. No one speaks. The dogs, their muzzles covered in blood, rub up against their masters' legs and perform carefree, risky slaloms, just short of causing the firm-jawed hunters to stumble.

The ice melts little by little and their boots slip on the muddy leaves. The forest opens and closes, from clearings to leafy tunnels. Nothing more can be heard other than the men's jerky breathing and the birds' disorderly and harmonic racket—trills and whistles, cackling and cooing. Do they understand each other? Tristan wonders, listening to the babel in the tall trees. He sticks his hand into his gamebag, strokes the rabbit's belly, feeling reassured by the touch of his fur, thinking that once the sun reaches its zenith, everything will be over, he will go back home, leave the mysterious world of virile fraternity for one much more familiar: the couple.

Living with a woman—isn't that what he has always known, after all? With his mother when he was growing up, and now with Emma. He knows too much about women's bodies and too little about men's. But he's going to learn. His determination is strong; it carries him with each step. He watches Dumestre, imitating his gait.

After a few hundred yards, the four hunters come to a halt. They've reached the overhang. They squat, kneel, and lie down in the undergrowth. Before their eyes, a green valley, similar to a vast pool of mist. They release the dogs. Without yapping, stealthy like their fox cousins, like their wolf brothers, they sink their delicate paws into the earth without disturbing a twig, without lifting a leaf. They start to encircle the area. Tristan dozes in the suspension of the moment. Nothing to do but wait.

And if the world stopped there, on the verge of killing, but without firing a bullet? Isn't this moment the best, the most fruitful? The perfection of the act in its conception. Doing inevitably means failing. Doing is destroying. For him, the idea is always preferable. That's what Emma criticizes him for. It's the reason she wants to leave him. I'm done, she says. With you, nothing is possible, we're not going anywhere. Love isn't enough. You have to fit in. She repeats this continuously, from morning to night, sometimes gently, often with cruelty. Fitting in, what's that?

It's living according to the laws of your species, the rabbit answers. It's doing what your instinct dictates. Take me, for example. I have three responsibilities: feeding myself, reproducing, escaping from predators. For you, it's more complicated: your lives are longer, as are your loves. I don't understand how you do it.

Me neither, thinks Tristan. But I haven't always been this lost. As a child, I used to soar along a clearly marked trajectory, a ball thrown into the air, with a clear kinetic gift.

You were following your instinct.

Exactly. When I was hungry, I'd eat; when I was tired, I'd sleep.

Did you want to break free?

No.

You should have.

Why?

Psst. Psst. Slowly, the rifles settle in the crooks of their shoulders. Suddenly, the dogs spring out from everywhere, barking. Immediately, the misty grass valley is lacerated with furry and feathered projectiles, chased out of their shelters, terrified. The deafening shots rip through the air. Tristan clamps his hands over his ears and watches the little bodies snatched up by nothingness in midflight. A few minutes later, the ground is strewn with the remains. The dogs fulfill their duty as undertakers. Docile, calm, hypnotized by their mindless domestic loyalty, they carry the carcasses to their masters, without licking up a drop of blood.

They're full, Tristan says to himself. The headless hen must've been fat.

No, says the rabbit. It's not that. They're trained. Trained to devour the scraps and bring back the catch. They never confuse the two, afraid of being beaten. For us, these are very strange creatures. They're not really animals, and yet not men either.

The hunters pat their doggies, congratulate themselves, smile, rub their hands together in satisfaction. Tristan imitates them.

It's time to uncork the wine, cut the dried sausage. Everyone chews. Tristan dreads conversation. Dumestre brings up public road maintenance, criticizes Peretti, who's on the town council, for not speaking up enough, for letting himself be bamboozled. The topic moves on to the mayor's secretary, her chest, then her handicapped son, which puts a damper on things. It takes four seconds for them to jump from this awkward subject to a banal one.

"Hey, this wine's not too bad!"

"Yeah, it's some good shit."

Tristan rolls himself a cigarette.

"Those things'll kill you, you know," says Farnèse, drinking straight from the bottle.

"Hey, boozer, nobody asked you," says Dumestre.

This is going to end badly, thinks Tristan, sticking his cigarette in his gamebag. He doesn't light it. The rabbit sniffs the tobacco, wrinkles his nose, sneezes. No one hears.

8

"You're scrubbing hard, right, sweetie? You do it like Mama told you. You know how Grandma likes when it's clean."

I'm scrubbing, thinks Tristan, rag in hand. His mother has never shown him how to scrub, but he understands this word. Thanks to context. Thanks to the imminent visit of Grandma. Grandma who is like Mama, but more... less...

At age six, he knows how to do everything in a house, and he does everything. The shopping, the cooking, the cleaning, the laundry. This goes in cold water, there's blood on it. This goes in hot water, there's grease. Their little apartment sparkles. Mama is lying on her bed. The ashes from her cigarette fall slowly onto the covers, drawing black halos, snags with burned borders like parchment that fascinate Tristan. He holds out an ashtray for her. She puts it on the nightstand and lights a new cigarette, its ashes falling on the bedspread. She swallows a pill. Takes a little drink. That's how she says it, "Just a little drink, to forget, so it hurts less. Do you want some candy?"

No. Tristan doesn't want candy. Never. Because of cavities, because of how much the dentist costs. He knows about everything. Sometimes he regrets having learned so much. When he was a baby, his mama took care of him, the house, the cooking. This isn't exactly the truth, but that's what he believes. One day, he did the vacuuming; the next day, the scrubbing. Then he was allowed to open cleaning products, to turn the dials on the gas range. With each one of his victories, his mother withdrew a bit more. After one or two years, Mama's territory was reduced to the square of her big bed. That's where she smokes. That's where she drinks. It's also where she cries, saying, "Oh, it's bad, it's bad for a mama to cry." Tristan forges her signature in his notebooks. Always good grades. Always first in his class. He has to be. With the smallest faux pas, his mother will be called in and that'll be the end of their little life together, their burrow, with the sun that comes in from the west and lights up the photo sitting on the chest of drawers, the one where Mama has long braids, a wide smile, and a flowery dress that's so stiff, so well ironed, you'd think it was made of cardboard.

In the end, Grandma doesn't come. Phew, everyone can breathe. Time to turn on the radio and listen to a few songs while eating potato chips.

9

"Here, take this," says Dumestre, walking through the brambles. He hands Tristan a partridge—elegant black coat with white spots. "That'll please your wife."

Tristan shakes his head.

"I can't accept it," he says, fearing that the immobile rabbit—probably asleep in his gamebag—would be crushed, horrified by the carcass on his back. "I didn't shoot it. That would be cheating."

"We always do this," insists Dumestre, resolute, jovial, continuing on his way. "We never know who shoots what, so we share, like brothers. Really, my pleasure."

Tristan feels it would be dangerous to refuse. He looks for a cover, a pretext. But suddenly, Dumestre disappears.

Midsentence, partridge in hand, he is swallowed up by the ground.

"Shit! Where'd he go?" cries Peretti, who was walking behind them.

They hear cracking noises, muffled sounds, a tumble, then nothing more, not one cry. For a moment, the three men remain at once speechless, amused, and horrified. It seems like a prank, a magic act. They can't believe their eyes. Farnèse rushes forward; Peretti pulls him back.

"Watch it, don't you fall too! It could be an old mine shaft. Dumestre!" shouts Peretti, still holding Farnèse by the sleeve. "Dumestre? Can you hear us? Say something. Fuck, Dumestre, say something."

Tristan, after twisting his gamebag around to his back in order to avoid crushing the rabbit, squats down and crawls toward the spot where Dumestre disappeared. With his arms out in front of him, he tests the terrain. The ground crumbles under his fingers.

"There's a hole," he says, looking at the other two.

"Go on, go a little farther," says Peretti, who has gotten down onto his knees to grab Tristan's feet. "I've got you. See if you can make anything out."

Tristan crawls forward cautiously, until his forearms are in the void. He lowers his head. A black tunnel opens up before his eyes. He doesn't know how deep it is; he can't see the bottom.

"So?" Farnèse inquires anxiously.

"I can't see anything," Tristan mutters. "You wouldn't happen to have a flashlight?"

"And why not a torch while you're at it," says Farnèse in a trembling, whimpering voice. "Oh, fuck. Fucking hell. This can't be happening."

"Stop your whining," orders Peretti. "We have to think. We can't panic."

Tristan, still hanging over the edge of the hole, listens carefully.

"Dumestre," he calls in a very gentle voice. "Dumestre? We're here. Don't worry. We're going to take care of you. Can you hear us? Dumestre?"

A groan rises from the depths of the earth. Weak, then stronger.

"He's alive," Tristan tells the other two. "He's alive. That's what counts. We're not going to panic. We'll call for help. They'll send a helicopter."

"How're you gonna call them?" asks Peretti. "We don't bring our phones when we go hunting. The last thing we need is our dear wives on our backs."

Tristan wiggles gently back out and stands up a few yards from the hole.

"I have my cell phone," he says with a smile. "It's fine."

"Shit," says Farnèse, hugging him. "Man, you're a hero. I have to say, I wasn't too thrilled about you coming in the beginning. After all, you're not from here, we don't know squat about you. But then, you pull out your phone. Shit, that's pretty great."

Tristan takes his phone out of his pocket, opens it, and realizes there's no service.

"Move, move," cries Peretti. "Go on, run over there, toward the clearing. It has to pick up a signal somewhere."

Tristan obeys and starts to run, phone in hand, checking the screen from time to time. He retraces his steps. Runs in another direction. Comes back. Starts again. Runs farther, panting.

In the gamebag, the rabbit wonders what the young man is up to. He recognizes the panic, the zigzagging, the desperate rush. Has he turned into a rabbit? What's gotten into him? Is he being pursued, hunted? Are there guns aimed at him? The rabbit would like to tell the young man that flight is futile, that it's better to wait, to lie low in the moss, without moving, almost without breathing.

After ten minutes of haphazard running, Tristan returns to his companions.

"We're wasting time," he tells them, out of breath. "If he's injured, we need to do something fast, as fast as possible. This isn't getting a signal anywhere. Go back to the car and get down to the village. Here, take my phone. As soon as you're on the main road, you'll be able to call. That's the best thing to do."

"The hero thinks he's a hero," mumbles Farnèse.

"What'd you say?" asks Peretti, teeth clenched. "I didn't hear that very well. What did you say?"

He points his rifle at Farnèse's thin chest. Farnèse steps back, trips over a root, falls backward.

"Nothing, I said nothing. Don't get all pissed off. Don't do something stupid."

Peretti lowers his weapon. "We have to calm down," he says. "Calm down, now. Let's go. You're right, kid. We'll go on foot. You stay here with Dumestre. Okay? Talk to him. Deal with this."

Tristan nods and watches the two men jog up the hill as they leave: Peretti, plodding along, as if the ground were sucking up the soles of his shoes; Farnèse, light and limping, like a wounded fawn. Around his neck, stirred up by the wind, a silk Indian scarf with a green-and-pink pattern unwinds its serpentine tail. Tristan notices this detail without dwelling on it. Hey, he says to himself, Farnèse is wearing a scarf, and something in this observation reso-nates like an enigma.

The sun has risen, imperceptibly warming leaves, branches, pebbles, skin.

Once Peretti and Farnèse are out of sight, Tristan sits on the ground and, very delicately, opens his gamebag. The rabbit's eyes, like two polished hazelnuts, stare at him.

"Today, you're the winner," he whispers, stroking the animal. "I'm going to free you."

He slips his hand under the animal's warm, soft, and supple stomach, touching the fragile, almost brittle ribs with the tips of his fingers.

"I'm gonna die," yells a voice from the bottom of the hole.

Tristan stuffs the rabbit back in his gamebag and closes it over him, then crawls once more toward the entrance of the tunnel.

"Dumestre? Dumestre? Help is on the way. Don't worry. It's fine. In twenty minutes, an hour at most. Are you hurt?"

"Shit, I'm gonna die."

10

"You think I'm gonna die, sweetie?" asks Mama, whose tiny body can barely be made out under the sheets. Only her arms, thin and dry like cut branches, her shoulders, narrow and bony, and her head, no more than a skull—sunken eye sockets, protruding cheekbones, chiseled jaw under her tight skin—are visible. "What do you say, honey? Can you give Mama a cigarette?"

Tristan lights a Dunhill Red without inhaling the smoke, which makes him nauseated, and brings it up to his mother's chapped lips. She sucks fearlessly. She no longer has the strength to eat or drink, only to draw on the filter. Tristan is sitting on the nightstand. His healthy, slender, muscular body and his soft, smooth bronze skin disgust him. He finds his body cumbersome; he would prefer to be a wisp of straw, like his mother, to drift along with her down the weakening stream of life. He closes his eyes. Shakes the ashes into the ashtray. Puts the cigarette between her eager lips once more.

"Shit, I'm gonna die," Mama murmurs in one breath. She starts coughing. The blood gushes from her mouth, her nose, as if her veins don't know how to contain it anymore, as if she were pierced with thousands of holes. Tristan dips a handkerchief into the bowl of water at the foot of the bed. He skims it over his mother's face, his fingers light as feathers, but she screams.

"You're hurting me! Don't press like that."

As he cleans her, she cries and says, "My big boy. Fifteen years old. How can you be fifteen? I was fifteen once. I was a knockout. You know that. Everyone does. A knockout, with her life ahead of her and men at her feet. Free, free, free. No one to put a leash on me. What fun I could have. People don't have fun like that today. Do you have fun? You're too serious. You only think about school. Did you already take the *baccalauréat*? No, it's too soon. Fifteen, that's young to take the bac exam. See, I never took it, so I have nothing to say. Oh, the fire! Can you see the big flames? I'm gonna go straight to hell. On a slide. Off I go, feetfirst. And you, you go and take your bac. Always so good. Too good. Always judging me. But with me, see, it was different. Teachers? Sons of bitches. Grades? Bitches. The system? A bitch. I wouldn't have it. But you, you do what you're supposed to. I never knew boys like you. Do boys like you even exist? Are there other ones like you at your school? I mean, exactly like you, who take the bac at fifteen, do the shopping, the cleaning, the laundry, and wipe their mothers. Ah, yes, that's true, it's not the same, it's not shit, it's blood, it doesn't come from the same place. It's more respectable. But now everything's the same for me. Up, down. Mouth, ass—same thing. That's the difference when you're dead. Hey, honey, I just made a big discovery. The difference when you're dead is that there are no more differences. So I'm dead. Am I dead, Tristan? Or not yet. Tell me not yet. You want to play a game of French tarot? Ah, no, shit, you can't do it with only two people. It's crazy how little you can do with two, don't you think? There's never been enough of us in this house. That's the problem. I should've done things totally different. But I wouldn't have wanted more children. Didn't want to be the mom with brats pulling on her skirt, the mom with her breasts hanging down. No. Something more like Snow White or Goldilocks. A girl—me—and seven dwarfs, or three bears. Some life, in fact. You don't add any life to this place. Since you were a baby, nothing. You never cried. Are you crying? You're crying because I'm gonna die. Shit, I'm gonna die. Five minutes ago, I was fifteen. Five minutes ago, I was a knockout."

11

Lying flat on his stomach on top of the leaves, Tristan inspects the silent hole. From time to time, he gently calls, "Dumestre?" No answer comes back up from the pit. He waits. He thinks.

Go down. Join Dumestre. Revive him. Carry him on your back. Go back up the slope with Dumestre's body that weighs one and a half times your own. Be a hero. Find the strength.

"Dumestre?"

The sun rises and Tristan starts to make out the contours inside the tunnel. Colors appear, melted together at first but growing more and more distinct as his vision adapts. He squints. It's like when you don't know how to read, and the letters, those indecipherable freight cars of the sentence train, file past and escape you.

Blood rushes into his tilted head. Dizziness overtakes his brain. Nausea in his stomach. In one bound, Tristan gets up, rubs his temples, breathes deeply. There's nothing to do. Just wait. The others must have reached the car.

Dumestre's car.

The key to Dumestre's car.

In the pocket of Dumestre's jacket.

At the bottom of the hole Dumestre fell into.

At what moment could they have realized? He's only just thought of it. He pictures them in front of the good old Citroën, the impenetrable, locked Citroën.

He imagines their feet kicking the tires, hears the swearing. You couldn't have thought of this, you dick-head? Dreads the fight. The loaded guns. The restless bullets. The relief of the blast. Sees them running, toward the road, making hand signals. The local highway is less than two miles away. They just need to run. In half an hour, they'll be there, attracting drivers, calling for help on the cell phone.

Be patient. Two hours instead of one. What's the difference?

12

Opera is so boring, thinks Tristan, age twelve, his hair styled like a model child's, sitting next to his mother, who is wearing a periwinkle-blue dress that is slightly too big for her and slightly too chic compared to her flat lace-up shoes. "I don't have any other ones. It doesn't matter. Who's going to see my feet? We'll be sitting down. We'll be in the dark."

They're sitting down in the dark, side by side, and on the stage, which is lit up from the wings and cluttered with red-painted traveling trunks, some women are singing, very loudly. They're too still, as if their arms have turned into sticks, their feet into boulders. From time to time, Tristan looks up at the supertitles and reads bits of sentences. It's a translation. His mother explained it to him. What's written above corresponds to what they sing below, but none of it makes sense. Tristan would like to leave, he'd like for all this to stop. He wants to climb up onto his seat and shout, Be quiet! Shake your hands out. Say something funny.

The boredom digs a sort of cave inside him, growing darker and vaster with every moment. On the walls, other, more familiar characters appear: the female cashier at Félix Potin who tousles Tristan's hair when he pays for the groceries—ever since he's grown taller, she's had to lift herself up off her seat a little bit to reach the top of his head, and when she sits back down, the cushion lets out a sort of sigh; Madame Tascaud, his French teacher, a substitute with long hair and lots of eye makeup, whose flat chest disconcerts him; Zadie Virlojeux, a tall junior who, they say, is sleeping with the assistant principal (old, so old, strict, ugly, navy-blue suit, dirty tie, how awful!); Lorette, the school nurse, who one day, while stroking his cheek for a while, said, "I know about your mama, okay?" (Know about what? he'd wanted to ask, but didn't dare, not wanting to risk hearing the answer); women, all kinds of women, with the cave walls like screens, but this isn't like at the movies, this is heavy, oppressive, fragmented. There isn't a story, he thinks, as though dealing with a personal insult.

His mother leans over and whispers in his ear: "Onegin and Lensky, two poets, best friends."

Why should I care?

He looks up in spite of everything to watch the creatures in wigs and starched collars who have just walked onstage. One is fat and sweaty, the other continuously swallowing his saliva, looking like he's about to vomit. Two poets, best friends. Okay. On the other side of the stage, two women: a hefty, rosy-faced one and a small one who's very pretty. Their lovers, thinks Tristan. Maybe something is going to happen. But no. They sing very loudly, as always, with their arms as straight as sticks. One of the women's voices is different. Suddenly, it's as if the inside of the cave, the vast cave of boredom, is lighting up.

Even though he wasn't expecting it, something grips his heart in a very pleasant way. An unknown word has grabbed on to a scale, the music swells, and the voice, which has captured his heart, turns him upside down like a snow globe, making the imprisoned white snowflakes twirl around inside the water-filled glass sphere. Russian, he thinks, is a sweet language, soaked with "*oo*" sounds that glisten like syrup.

He dozes off and scratches his knee through his corduroy pants, lulled by the tiny sound his nail makes against the rough fabric. The cave plunges into darkness once more. His breath slows. He falls asleep.

When he wakes up, the stage is strewn with white-painted traveling trunks. The two men, the poets, best friends, are facing each other. What are they doing with pistols in their hands? Tristan looks up at his mother's face and sees her tears flowing, framing a smile. He watches her chin as it traces a tiny circle in one direction, then in the other. More of an eight than a circle, as if her head were dancing imperceptibly on her neck. She closes her eyes, smiles more, places her two hands flat on the silky fabric of her dress.

The action has shifted. Now only his mother's body dances immovably to the chords whose complex harmony convinces Tristan of... he doesn't know what. Exaltation, jubilation, the senses overtaking the brain. He's not used to not understanding.

A shot. The fat one has fallen backward. He's dead. Two poets, best friends. One killed the other.

13

"Here's what we're going to do," Tristan says to Dumestre, who doesn't respond, who might be dead at the bottom of the hole, with his car keys buried in his jacket pocket. "I'm going to come down very slowly. I'm going to get closer."

Tristan makes it up as he goes along. He can't see how to put this improvised plan into action. Words come out of his mouth, like a charmed snake.

"I'm going to feel my way there, hands in front of me"—and saying it, he does it—"head down. I'll hang on to the roots," and saying it, he does it. "There, that's good, it's not too steep. I can't see anything, but I think I can hear you breathing. That's good. Don't panic. I can hear you. You're on my right, I think, a little to the right. Yes, there, I'm putting my hand on a rock. It's steady. Like stairs. There, I'm crawling. Hanging on with my feet too," and saying it, he does it. "Ow, nicked my finger. Nothing serious. I'm still coming. Don't move, whatever you do. Don't try anything. I'm the one coming to you. Trust me. I can hear you better and better. Can you talk? Say something.

That'll help me move toward you. Mind you, I don't really have a choice. It's cramped down here. Don't worry, I'm not going to fall on you."

The tunnel narrows, then widens, levels out. A reflection ricochets off a wall. Dumestre's watch has captured a beam of sunlight that snuck in who knows how, from who knows where. With his gamebag on his stomach, Tristan now moves forward on his backside, heels in front. The rabbit is in his element. The plan is his idea. In case of danger, there's nothing better than a burrow. It's cool in the summer and warm in the winter. As long as you're in a burrow, there's nothing to worry about. The young man is his first student. An apprentice who, though lacking in agility, makes up for it with caution. There's nothing to fear in the earth. We start and end our days in it. It's a trusted ally. A source of comfort.

As for this old mine shaft, the rabbit knows all of its nooks and crannies. Many galleries lead to it. Those hollowed out in the past by men have long since collapsed, which leaves the other ones, dug out by animals, each with his own technique: gnawers, scrapers, burrowers. In certain places, narrow, vertical channels lead to the surface, like chimneys. He doesn't know who created this masterpiece. It's through here that the morning sun, leaping to and fro, full of cunning, has slipped down to position itself on the glass face of the watch, as precise as a lacemaker's needle.

"Okay, almost there. Say something. No, it's okay, don't talk. Don't wear yourself out. I'm coming. Really slowly. You can't fall any farther. My eyes have adjusted to the darkness. Hey, there we go, I can see you. Your gun is shining. Your watch. I'm touching your hair."

"Fucking hell, kid," grumbles Dumestre. "Don't enjoy it."

Tristan slides down next to Dumestre. He'd like to hug him but knows that he shouldn't.

"Are you hurt?"

"What do you think?"

"You had quite a fall. But it's okay. You're alive. That's what counts."

"I don't hurt," moans Dumestre. "I don't hurt anywhere. I can't feel anything."

"What do you mean?"

"I can't feel my legs or my arms. I can feel my head, that's it. You know what that means?"

Tristan doesn't answer.

"It means a vegetable in a wheelchair. Oh, fuck, this can't be happening."

"No, it's the shock," says Tristan. "Farnèse and Peretti went to get help. We're going to pull you out of here."

"I'm buried alive. Shit."

Tristan doesn't know how to respond. He slides his hand into his gamebag, makes sure that the rabbit is still alive too. The animal nibbles on his finger.

"You're gonna get me out of here," Dumestre mutters. "You hear me? I'm not staying here like an idiot in a hole. You better figure it out. You get me up there, if not I'll beat the crap outta you."

Tristan knows that Dumestre can't do anything to him. With paralyzed arms and legs, he's at his mercy.

"I think it would be better if you stay still," he says. "If the spinal cord is affected...I've heard that somewhere... that you should never move an injured person."

"I'm not an 'injured person.' I'm the guy who's gonna beat you to a pulp if you don't get me out of this hellhole. You do what I say. Fuck, I need to piss."

"Oh, that's a good sign!" Tristan exclaims. "That means... well, you know. That's what I was thinking. It's the shock, but the spinal cord isn't affected, otherwise—"

"Spare me the anatomy lesson, kid. Do what I tell you. You get me out of here. And fast. I don't want to piss on myself."

Tristan studies the sides of the hole. He peers up the narrow chimney through which the sunlight is coming to land on the watch's glass face. Looks back behind him where he came from, examines the slope he went down. Thinks. He seems to remember that the ground above them inclined steeply from where the hole was. He notes that the distance between them and the light directly over their chests is less than the distance he crawled in his descent. He draws a triangle in his head, calculates without numbers, nothing but the help of mental pictures, of illuminated points of impact, pretending to be Pythagoras.

"We're going to get out through the bottom," he explains.

"What kind of bullshit is this? You trying to get me trapped?"

"No, no. It's too steep at the top. I'll risk hurting you if I carry you. And I'm not even sure if I actually can carry you."

"When you have to save a man, believe me, you can carry twice your weight. When you kill an animal, a big one, it's the same. Whatever the weight, a man can carry it on his back. The other week, I bagged a gorgeous one with these big, beautiful princess eyes. Shot him right in the heart. Didn't spoil anything. A beaut. And I carried him on my own, right to the car. I don't know how much he weighed, but when I put my arm under him, I was already short of breath. Then I lifted him over my head and brought him back on my shoulders. We have a lot more strength than we think, you know. We're just afraid of getting hurt."

Tristan tries picturing the handsome male with princess eyes. He doesn't even know which species it was; Dumestre didn't specify and Tristan doesn't dare ask. He imagines them, man and animal, like the illustrations in the Greek mythology book he used to look through as a kid. Gods, demigods, mortals—it was all so well organized. How sad to give it up. No one believes in that anymore, he'd been told. But it's so logical, so orderly, he had retorted—he must have been five or six years old. They'd laughed at his naïveté. But what about God, the God of the church, he had added, are there still people who believe in that? The laughter grew quiet. He had made a mistake. He didn't really know what it was. He had made someone angry. He had made everyone angry. But it was logical: if no one believed in the Greek gods, even though they were so interesting, so meticulously described, so cunning, so powerful, what good was it to believe in another one—singular, newer, more modern, certainly, but so much sadder? He had never brought it up again. He had accurately pinpointed the impropriety of his thoughts.

It was one of those times when he and his mother had been invited to Vigie. Vigie was the name of the village or the house, he didn't know. A big square yellow building with a double spiral staircase, columns, floors that glistened like lakes, vases with no flowers in them, long-legged dogs who would come and drool on the plates with gold borders and navy-blue monograms, on the silverware, the napkins, big tough squares like bedsheets that were heavy on your knees and that absolutely must not be used to wipe your mouth.

On the train that took them there, Mama made him repeat the lesson. Silverware: always from outside to inside. Napkin: as white at the end of the meal as it was at the beginning. Elbows: off the table. Hands: never in your lap. Please. No thank you. Yes, I'd love some. Bread: don't touch. Conversation: listen, smile, don't speak except to answer a question. You remember the last time, what a fuss! Gaze: rather low, somewhere between the tablecloth and the speaker's chin. Tristan knew it by heart, but he would repeat the lesson to his mother, her eyes lost in the distance on the other side of the train window, who was the most beautiful woman in the world. At the train station, a car was waiting for them. Mama gave courteous kisses to the chauffeur on his cheeks before climbing in the backseat in a rustle of silk.

Once the car door slammed in the driveway, Mama didn't say good-bye to the uniformed man, didn't look at him. On the front steps, a gentleman and a lady—he an owl; she a turkey—opened their arms wide with two identical smiles. The Parisians! they exclaimed. A second later, the enthusiasm subsided. They coldly shook hands. The emotion had worn everyone out.

Just before lunch—long and solemn, during which, in spite of everything, you didn't have time to eat anything—

Astre, a little girl who had brown eyes with dark rings under them, a yellowish complexion, pale lips, and hair pulled back so tightly into her ballet bun that her eyebrows and eyelids lengthened toward her temples like a Chinese mask, asked him in the hallway, "Have you read this? It's great stuff!" while, from under her skirt, she took out a magazine whose title he couldn't manage to decipher. At age six, he knew how to read, but he was too distracted by the booklet's appearance and disappearance under her little-girl plaid skirt to concentrate. Without waiting for his answer, she skipped in front of him—just enough time to make her kilt dance—before quickly going back to her senator's gait, chin out, shoulders back, which made her look just like the turkey hostess.

Was Astre his cousin? Was Astre pretty? Was he in love with her?

In the train compartment, his mother had made him repeat the guests' names: Uncle Évariste, Aunt Cyprienne, Cousin Luc, Cousin Paul, Little Léon, Little Lollet, Vava and Mimi, Jeanne-Christelle, Astre, Amaury, Georgina, Darling Paul, Darling Cyprienne, Baby Louise, Baby Véronique, the twins, Arthus and Jean-Christophe; and then the friends, of course: Dodo, the prefect, Irène, Gégé, Loulou, the duchess. The faces he associated with this garland of names were more or less similar to those of the characters in the game of Clue. The young ladies and the little girls had the face of Miss Scarlet; the impressive, white-haired gentlemen, that of Colonel Mustard, and so on.

When he really wanted to suck his thumb at the table, or when he felt his back, which he wasn't allowed to rest against his chair, start to dangerously slouch, he would recite to himself the litany of names that had never been synonymous with family.

How many times had they gone for lunch at Vigie? Two, maybe three. But it quickly becomes easy to think of an exceptional excursion as something normal when you have only a few years of experience on the earth. Tristan thought they'd be going there for their entire lives, that he would get married to Astre, and, one day, they'd be opening their arms wide on the front steps to welcome "the Parisians."

But there had been a scandal.

The word used to make Mama laugh until she cried. A scandal! Ha ha ha! she'd exclaim. Almost as hilarious as when Tristan had asked her who his father was. Your father! Ha ha ha! I have absolutely no idea, really, not one!

The scandal. Mama, on the train. Not quite as beautiful, constantly moving, fragile, divided. The dress that gapes open at her chest and rides up on her knees. The weak, glazed-over look. A small, strange smile. At the table, a sleeve that comes up the moment she extends her arm to reach for the wine carafe—"Come now, Love, Éloi is going to serve you." Love was the name they had given to her at Vigie. Tristan would call her Mama, other people called her Madame Rever. Her ID card said Amandine Bartole de La Houssaye.

The sleeve that rides up attracts stares—there's something in the hollow of her elbow. Mama doesn't listen to what they're saying to her; she knocks over one glass, then two. She wants that wine. Why? Anyone's guess. It's her grail. She grabs it. Drinks right from the carafe.

"Didine!" shouts the prefect.

On the train ride back, Tristan studies his mother's arms. He contemplates the little red dots.

"Does it hurt?" he asks.

She trembles a little.

"Do you like those people?" she asks. "I hate them. We're not going there anymore."

Tristan thinks of Astre, who, though a brunette with brown eyes, becomes inscribed in his memory as a blonde with blue eyes, like Miss Scarlet in the original version of Clue.

14

Tristan has been digging straight in front of himself, under Dumestre's stream of insults. With his hands, with his feet. The rabbit helped him. Whatever you do, don't think about it, just throw yourself into the earth like you would into water, into the air. All the elements are equal. Don't estimate what's left to accomplish, don't congratulate yourself for what's already been done. Dig for the pleasure of it, forgetting that necessity is what drives us. Dig for the sweet, sharp smell that emerges with each swipe of your paws. Go for it with your eyes closed, feeling confident, armed with nothing but your joy. Keep your body tight, act as though the earth is opening itself up, on its own initiative, moved by its desire to welcome you in. Provoke this desire. Make yourself long, make yourself soft.

There, that's good, that's it, exactly, there you go.

The rabbit is becoming more and more satisfied with his student. He appreciates how docile he is, how flexible his body is. But one thing annoys him: he doesn't understand why Dumestre is shouting, or why Tristan is saving him.

Let the fat one die. He's injured and angry—he won't hold up for long.

We don't do that. We don't let people die.

A mother for her young, okay. Is the shouting fat one your child? (The question is sincere. The rabbit is unaware of everything, or almost everything, to do with human life and reproduction.)

No, he's not my child, but we belong to the same species. He's my brother, if you like. My human brother.

If you were the one who was injured, the shouting fat one would save you too?

He would save me too. That's how it is with us.

How touching, says the rabbit. No, "touching" isn't the right word. It's beyond the words I know. It's something I can't understand, something I can hardly grasp. Is it what you humans call love?

No.

You're sure?

Absolutely sure.

"What are you doing, digging another tunnel under the English Channel?" Dumestre yells. "I need to piss. It's not like I'm waiting around for you to smuggle us across some fucking border. Shit, I just want to get out. See the sky."

Tristan wonders if he still has his fingernails. He's afraid the earth might have torn them off his fingertips at some point. He continues nonetheless. The soil is becoming looser, mixed with pebbles and leaves—he's almost there.

His right thumb is the first to shoot out. The feeling of the outside air on his skin elates him and doubles his strength. He pulls his arms in alongside his body and plows headlong into the dirt, pushing with his feet, head forward, eyes shut, mouth closed, breath held, like a human cannonball, like a baby. His face suddenly bursts forth from the hill. No one can see this incongruous cameo, the colors almost tone on tone because Tristan's skin has turned brown from the dust and mud. Only the relief of his nose and his blue eyes looking out over the valley distinguish him from the exposed, knotted roots just a few yards away. He breathes in. He smiles. He's afraid.

The rest of his body is behind him, inaccessible. He's cut off from it, can't see it, and is uncertain of whether he can still feel it. He gently moves one hand, then the other, fearing he might knock down the tunnel he's just dug. He'll have to back in, turn around inside, and make the opening bigger. He is overcome with fatigue, a rapid and full equinoctial tide, wiping away everything in its path. He is overcome with a limp feeling, like an infant being lulled to sleep.

"The fuck you doing, goddammit?!"

Moving his arms away from his neck as much as possible, Tristan slowly pushes himself back toward the interior of the earth while preserving the porthole of daylight cut out by his head.

"It's fine," he says in an almost inaudible voice. "We're going to make it, I promise."

Back in the hole once more, he checks to see if the rabbit is breathing. He could have crushed him during that last push. But the rabbit's heart is still beating. His muzzle stirs.

"Where's Newspaper?" Dumestre suddenly asks in a distraught voice.

Newspaper is Dumestre's dog, a springer spaniel. On the day Dumestre introduced him to Tristan, he took more care than he'd taken in speaking about his children, two boys (one an IT specialist, the other a manager of a sporting goods store, both big wigs). Dumestre called him Newspaper because it wasn't a common name, and also because the dog brings him his newspaper in the evening, when he gets home from work.

"Newspaper, ya like that?" Dumestre had asked him. "For a dog, I mean?"

"Yeah, that sounds nice. It's not too long or too short."

"It's not pretentious either," Dumestre remarked, tenderly petting the dog's head, which was white with ginger spots. "This dog, he's... how can I say it? He's me, except he's a dog."

Their friendship, if that's what you could call the restless and furtive feeling that unites them, was born that day, at that moment, around that confession. Because Dumestre had found the courage to say it and Tristan hadn't made fun of him.

"Yeah, I get it. You understand him and he understands you."

"Shit, kid, I like you." To Newspaper: "I like him. Should we have a drink?"

Following Emma's suggestion, Tristan had gone to ask Dumestre to borrow a tool.

"It's a pretext," she had explained to him. "You have to make contact. The rest will follow."

That was three years ago.

It took three years for Dumestre to finally invite him to go hunting.

15

In London, things had been different. He and Emma had both been strangers. Their status was clear: they were tolerated. Everything was allowed, because no matter what they did, there was no question of integrating. Tristan had stopped going to class rather quickly. They had to make money to support themselves. Emma's salary wasn't enough. He was eighteen years old. Everything in his life was happening too fast. He felt like someone had sped up the wheel of time and his existence was playing out in fast-forward.

This disturbance dated precisely back to his mother's death, which happened the day after the last test for the *baccalauréat*. He had immediately received a letter from the person she used to call "our benefactor," with a hint of mockery in her voice. The prefect (was that really his job? was it a nickname?) was watching over them. The opera tickets, for example, had been his gift.

He was the one who took care of the funeral. Ashes spread in the Memorial Garden.

"Benedetti's Schumann," he whispered in Tristan's ear. "So beautiful. A must."

So sad, thought Tristan. Gloomy. Sinister. Mama's death wasn't like that. Mama's death was "Summertime" by Janis Joplin.

The pale rain drew awkward arabesques on the ground.

"Does the young man wish to scatter the ashes himself?" asked the funeral home attendant, a thirtysomething man who spoke with a lisp and was exhibiting excessive politeness.

I've carried her so often, thought Tristan.

The urn was heavy; this wasn't her, this dense mass, this opaque matter. He would've loved to tell the mortician and the prefect—the only two witnesses to the scene—about the particular lightness that had taken over his mother's body in the last days. A twig, a leaf, the seedlings of a dandelion, no more mass, a body that let light filter through, a strainer, a wire fence, a cheesecloth. She had become immaterial and translucent. Only her laugh still had some flesh to it.

Of the days, weeks, and months that follow, almost nothing remains. The sounds of feet, of boxes, the smell of cardboard. Tristan obeys the orders he receives by phone, by mail. He spends the summer near Bordeaux. Helps with the grape harvests. The owner of the vineyard is one of the prefect's friends. Sometimes he invites Tristan to the winemakers' table. Tristan refuses with a smile. Everyone is relieved (The kid's just lost his mother, they whisper, shaking their heads). The other boys don't speak to him. They smoke, bare-chested, at the top of the hillside, dazed by fatigue, by the sun, mentally recounting the money earned from breaking their backs.

Tristan picks up a fallen cigarette from between two vine shoots. He asks the least hostile of his colleagues for a light. He inhales. Mama!

He buys a pack of Dunhill Reds at the *tabac* in the village. The ashes, he thinks, I'll never be finished scattering her ashes.

He reads a book he found among her things. He doesn't remember slipping it in his suitcase. It's a little volume with a sky-blue silk cover that fits in his pocket. During each break, in the morning while drinking his coffee, in the evening while eating dinner, and, later, in bed, he turns the pages. It's his first time reading a book for himself. He's intimidated. Mama always wanted him to read the newspaper. He would carry out the task in a loud, clear voice. She appreciated his diction, made comments, assured him that if he was well informed, he would have the means to steer his life in the right direction, to not allow himself to be cheated, to take control.

"Will we read the crime stories too?"

"We'll read everything! It's important to know what man is capable of. Rape, theft, murder—all that's written in our DNA. Does that scare you?"

"No."

And he would read all these sentences that stuck to the edges of his brain. It was the murmur of the world, of course, but he didn't join in and never would.

The little blue book is very different; it has a special power. Up until now, the books he read (always for school, never for pleasure) would at best leave traces in his mind, inhabiting his memory. This story doesn't force its way in. Quite the opposite—Tristan is the one who enters the paper, loses himself in it, dissolves in it. There are monsters, mermaids, beasts with a hundred eyes, chasms, animals that talk, enchanted rivers. It's his domain. One second is all he needs. He opens to a page, no matter which one, and his eyes have hardly settled on the words before he's swallowed up.

He doesn't talk about it. What would he say? He doesn't know if it's normal. He realizes that his mother, in wanting to prepare him for the worst, neglected to teach him ordinary things.

At the end of the summer, he is driven to the airport in the prefect's car. LONDON-HEATHROW blinks on a display board. He will stay with Mrs. Klimt, at Seven Sisters. He will receive a certain sum via money order every month. He will take classes at a language school: foundational courses. The year is taking shape before his eyes, scattered with constraints, novelties, rules. The prefect has prepared everything, written everything down.

"This notebook," he says to Tristan while entrusting it to him, "is your vade mecum. Did you study Latin? Well, it doesn't matter. Let's just say it's like the Game of the Goose. If you follow each page to the letter, like moving your piece forward on the squares, I'll come to your graduation ceremony in four years and we'll celebrate at the Savoy. All the oysters and champagne you want."

Tristan frowns. He doesn't really know how to play the Game of the Goose, but he remembers one time in grade school when he had landed on jail and stayed there until the game was over.

Seven Sisters. In spite of his rudimentary English, Tristan knows what it means. How can this be the name of a metro station or a neighborhood? Who were the seven sisters, and how could he, an only child, get there? Over the course of his journey by train, then by subway, then by bus, he imagines seven girls with ash-blond hair, pale pink lips, freckles on pointed noses, long hands, and plump feet.

At each bus stop, he asks the driver if it's the place where he should get off. The man, who is wearing a cap and has big tufts of red hair sprouting out of his ears, patiently shakes his head, until the moment when he finally nods, which Tristan takes as a sign of agreement, a silent benediction.

On the sidewalk, he consults the hand-drawn map on page 3 of the notebook. Turns it in one direction. In another. The clumps of grass growing between the cobblestones glisten in the sunlight. The sky above, sprinkled with little chubby clouds, is slowly turning pink.

"Excuse me, where the street?"

Tristan points to his map. He is talking to a woman wearing a scarf around her head, who puts her shopping bag on the ground, takes out her glasses, holds her chin in her hand, studies the drawing while coughing violently, looks right, left, smiles at Tristan, and gives him back his notebook without another word.

She walks away, slowly, without turning back around.

Tristan's throat tightens. He doesn't understand where he is, doesn't speak English, doesn't understand who these people are or where they're going. No one knows he exists; no one cares about him. He could disappear. He feels so tiny that a crack in the road would be enough to swallow him up. He's cold. He's hungry. He's tired. He needs to pee. He's alone in the world.

Emma often tells him, "You're alone. You can't do anything about it. That's what you know best. You're at home in solitude." Emma strings together expressions that all mean the same thing, like reproaches washing over him that she says again and again, as though waiting for him to ask her for forgiveness.

16

They look like two survivors of a volcanic eruption.

Their clothes are torn, covered in mud, their faces and hands powdered with soil.

They're lying down, side by side, on the hill, regaining their breath.

Tristan feels like he's achieved something, but this achievement is nothing compared to what awaits them.

After having gone back down into the tunnel, he widened the opening, went out again to study the terrain, the slope that was going to welcome them. It was fine. Any steeper and they would slide to the bottom of the valley, whereas here, a sort of false flat, a terrace hanging over the vast basin of green grass, had been shaped by destiny.

Tristan seized Dumestre by the ankles and pulled, gently.

"Pull harder!" shouted Dumestre. "Faster! What the hell are you doing? I'm not made of glass. Besides, I can't feel anything—I'm already broken. Hurry up! My mouth is full of dirt. It's gonna collapse up there. I'm gonna piss myself. Dammit, kid, give a good tug!"

So, with all his might, supporting himself with his knees and his feet, Tristan grabbed Dumestre's boots and braced himself at the mouth of the hole to pull his companion free.

He had hardly gotten him out when the gallery that had been sheltering them collapsed in on itself, with the groan of a dying animal.

Who's going to speak now? What are they going to say to each other?

Tristan feels overcome with an incredible shyness.

"What time is it?" Dumestre asks softly.

Tristan looks at his watch. "Noon."

"Noon? Shit, we've been here for hours. What the hell are they doing?"

They're kicking the tires of the impenetrable Citroën, thinks Tristan. They're cursing at each other, fighting, one shot rings out, then another. They're killing each other.

"I don't know," he says. "Maybe they had a hard time finding the road."

"Undo my fly, kid. I don't have hands or arms anymore. I need to piss."

Ah, Tristan thinks. Of course. Undo his fly. He doesn't have hands or arms, but...

Putting his weight on his elbow, he leans over Dumestre's body, undoes his belt and the three buttons, and waits. For what exactly, he doesn't know.

"You can't do things halfway, dickhead. You think the cuckoo's going to come out of the clock all by itself?"

Ah, Tristan thinks once more. Of course. The cuckoo.

With his eyes looking far, far toward the horizon, he forages in his disabled companion's pants. His fingers don't belong to him anymore. Rough cotton, soft jersey, smooth skin like a baby's eyelid. There. That's done, it wasn't a big deal after all. He gently turns Dumestre's body to the side so the man doesn't wet himself, and, while listening to the solemn, ringing song of the hot stream on the wilted leaves, he watches the sky, which has suddenly changed color over the hill, there in the east, which overlooks and conceals the village. -

Dumestre lets out a big, deep sigh and falls back with all his weight, disheveled, cuckoo still out.

"What the heck is that color?" says Tristan, looking at the sky.

From where they are, on their miraculous balcony, they can see the heavens sliced cleanly in two. Above their heads, it's bright blue and a brilliant white sun; on the opposite side, just a few miles away, it's iron gray dotted with black droplets, the light swallowed up by a rift, into which pours a muddled ink, suddenly stupefied by the starving grimace of a voltaic arc.

"The end of the world," Dumestre declares in an indifferent voice.

Tristan thinks of Emma.

An arrow bursts from his distraught mind, planting itself at the entrance of their house. A shack foolishly perched, as though stunned, on a field, with no lightning rod on top. The roof is missing some shingles. The beams sag wearily, ashamed of the building's ugliness. The doorframes are loose. There are so many drafts that, even in calm weather, a forgotten leaf can fly away on its own. Our haunted castle, they call it, laughing to ward off the fear that the house might collapse on them one day.

A dull, low roar, a furious belch, the lazy growl of a dragon awoken from his sleep makes the earth tremble.

"Six seconds," says Dumestre. "Right on the village."

"What're you talking about?" Tristan asks.

"The storm," Dumestre says in a weary voice, like an exasperated schoolteacher speaking to a dunce. "Six seconds between the lightning and the thunder. Light travels faster than sound. Didn't they teach you anything in school? That shit you see over there is already falling on them. In a few minutes, if the wind direction doesn't change, it'll be on us."

Tristan looks around. Down below, not the least bit of shelter. Upward is the hill, and above that, probably the forest, but from where he is, he can't see anything but an abrupt, bare rise, a mound deformed by the recent collapse, probably filled with craters and cavities.

"The end of the world," Dumestre repeats, and he laughs softly.

"I think..." hazards Tristan. "Well, I read somewhere... I heard that the thing to do in a thunderstorm is flatten yourself against the ground. That way you don't attract lightning."

"Well, as for me," says Dumestre, "I don't have a choice. Here I am, flat on the ground."

"You still can't feel anything?" Tristan asks, worried.

"Do up my fly, will ya?"

Tristan complies. Now it's like he's used to doing it. For some things, once is enough.

"What about your legs, your arms?" Tristan insists. "Still nothing?"

"At this point," answers Dumestre, "what does it matter?"

"Try, at least. A finger, a toe?"

"Don't panic, kid, I'm screwed," Dumestre says, and he starts laughing like a madman, like a monster.

I won't panic, thinks Tristan. At worst, we'll be soaked. We'll wait for it to pass. Thunderstorms never last long. It's only water.

Water, thinks the rabbit. Lots of water knocking down unstable ground in one stroke. Water mixes with the earth, turns into mud, torrents of mud. A heavy brown avalanche carrying everything away with it. A thick river without a bed, overflowing, thirsting for speed; an unstoppable river that drags away everything—trees, houses, cars, men, animals.

"Tell me a story," says Dumestre.

17

That's strange, Tristan thinks. And as if it were an equation to solve, he mentally notes: an ailing body without strength, a desperate situation, the threat of death... I do what I'm told, I follow orders, I'm the nurse, the maid. But in one instance, it's my mother, and in the other, Dumestre. In one instance, it's a woman; in the other, a man.

Get me out of this, tell me a story, light a fire, light a cigarette, tell me I'm not going to die, find shelter. The situations are similar, but the impact is different, as if the voice giving the orders isn't speaking to the same organ. One to the heart, the other to the brain. At the moment, Dumestre is like my father, older than me, bigger, more fearsome, quick-tempered, impatient. That's a discovery. I feel as though by staying here alone with him, in the wilderness that's decided to engulf us, I'll finally have a taste of what a father is, seeing as I've never had one. I like it... and I don't.

A father? asks the rabbit. What's that?

It's the male who got your mother pregnant.

Never saw him, the rabbit answers. Never heard of him.

There wasn't a male figure around you or your mother while you were growing up?

No. What's a father for?

Giving orders, teaching you the rules, Tristan says without thinking.

So he's good for nothing, the rabbit replies. Where I come from, there are no rules. We don't need them. Instinct, good luck, and bad luck are the three pillars of our miserable existence.

A father, Tristan thinks while watching Dumestre, trying to fully feel the harsh contact, the relationship's suppressed violence.

"Tell me a story," repeats Dumestre. "Like you would to your kid."

"I don't have children," Tristan answers.

"I know," says Dumestre. "So, like when you were a kid and your mother would tell you a story."

"My mother?" Tristan says, and he bursts out laughing, doubles over, in tears, his belly aching.

"What about your mother?"

Tristan laughs even harder. He puts his hand in his gamebag, on the rabbit's back, to try to calm down. Takes a breath, lets out little high-pitched cries.

"She's dead," he says finally. "A long time ago. I had just turned sixteen."

"She couldn't have been that old," Dumestre remarks. "Was it an accident?"

"No."

"Then what? How'd your mother die?"

And as if it were a fairy tale, a children's story, Tristan begins: "Once upon a time, there was a little girl named Astre."

"That's a pretty name," interrupts Dumestre. "So that's it, your mother's name was Astre? Well, that's a good start."

"No, my mother's name was Amandine."

"Well then?" Dumestre protests.

"I'm starting from the end," Tristan declares. "Sometimes it's better, for suspense, to start from the end."

18

Mrs. Klimt's house smells like fried food and cloves. As soon as Tristan enters the front hall—painted a shade of bottle green and so dimly lit that he can hardly distinguish the outline of the woman who has just opened the door—his throat is seized with the nauseous aroma. A cascade of "wilshwarwer'nswishdilworn" beats down on him. It's English. The language that Mrs. Klimt speaks and that he doesn't understand. She turns on the light, takes his hands in hers, looks at him, takes a step back, as if to study him, and leans over to grab the handle of his suitcase.

"No, no, not touch. *Très lourd!*" he exclaims to spare the old lady from breaking her back.

She has blue eyes, white hair, high, rosy cheekbones, hollow cheeks, a pointy chin, and slightly protruding teeth. Tristan finds her very pretty, but he doesn't know if it's possible to think this, to think of an old lady as being pretty. The only one he knew was Grandma, and Grandma had dyed blond hair and wore lots of makeup and perfume. In the end, it was as if she no longer had an age or a face. Or a body. A mass of perfume. Rigidity and saturation.

She's still alive. Didn't come to her daughter's funeral. Didn't see fit to take care of her grandson. After the Vigie scandal, at which she hadn't been present, but which someone or other had related to her, Grandma blew a gasket.

"Burn this for me, son," Mama said, holding out a ball of paper to Tristan.

"What is it?"

"Your grandmother's death sentence. A letter. I've read it, now you burn it, and we'll never speak of it again. She's gone from my life. She's gone from yours."

"What did she write?"

"Malicious things, false claims, curses."

"Won't you miss her?"

"No."

"What about when you were little?"

"What?"

"Was she nice when you were little?"

"I don't remember. I don't remember anything about my childhood."

And, without knowing why, Tristan felt personally affected by this confession. As though it threatened his own childhood, as if his mother hadn't saved anything for him. Out of selfishness, out of cruelty.

Mrs. Klimt shows him his room upstairs. Thick blue carpeting on the uneven, creaking floor; a bench seat covered with turquoise chintz; paintings on the walls, gold-framed landscapes with waterfalls, horses and wistful knights; a chest of drawers as heavy as an ocean liner; a dark wood bed, up on risers, covered with a paisley duvet.

Tristan has never seen anything more cozy.

Mrs. Klimt leaves him after uttering an incomprehensible, enthusiastic phrase. She closes the door.

Tristan is alone, his bladder hurts, hunger is crushing his stomach, but he can't figure out how to resolve these three afflictions.

What could she have said?

Good night, see you tomorrow.

Please don't bother me.

Come have dinner in five minutes.

The bathroom is at the end of the hallway.

How could he know?

How can he avoid committing a faux pas?

He sits on the bed, which bends under his light teenage frame and nearly closes up on him, like an anemone, a nest.

Other people before me have gone through this. The uprooting, the solitude, the confusion, the fear of doing something wrong. Still, the worst would be getting the duvet or the carpet dirty. For a second, he considers pissing out the window, but he can't see how to open the two horizontal panes. No handle, no latch. Nothing. Smooth wood and two thick ropes on the sides that seem to go into the framework and don't slide. A prison.

Tristan musters his courage, the pain in the hollow of his stomach assisting him. Without making any noise, he opens the door, looks right, left, bets on the end of the hallway, chooses the door on the right; his bladder relaxes, he feels the relief, the release in advance. But no, it's a closet. Door at the end, locked; door to the left, another bedroom.

He groans so that he doesn't cry. As long as Mrs. Klimt doesn't hear him. As long as no one ever knows what provoked that sob.

A voice comes up from the ground floor, an inquisitive, singsongy, cheerful voice.

Too bad. There, on the side table, a vase. But first, try the last door. Victory! Blessed black-and-white linoleum, the kind you want to kneel down on and kiss, in prostration before the promised land—the bathroom!

A few minutes later, emboldened, revived, he heads for the kitchen. Mrs. Klimt is waiting for him. She designates a teapot, a loaf of gray bread the size of a piglet, a saucer on which glistens a very white, very soft kind of butter, along with a board where an enormous, apparently indestructible orange cube sits enthroned.

"Fro-mage!" she enunciates with a great deal of care.

It's one of the only French words she knows. She presses her hand to her mouth, does a U-turn, rushes toward the fridge, and takes out a cluster of muscat grapes while royally announcing, *"La rai-son!"*

Tristan thanks her in English, wondering if it's appropriate to help himself.

But she disappears, furtively, without another word, without leaving him the choice.

This bread, this soft white butter, and this indestructible cheese are, beyond a doubt, the best things he's ever eaten. Overcome with gratitude, incapable of expressing it, he puts everything away and cleans up once his meal is finished.

Mrs. Klimt bolts into the kitchen right when he's in the middle of scrubbing the teapot's tannin-stained interior with the sponge. Poor old lady, she no longer has the strength to scour...

Mrs. Klimt lets out a cry. Or rather, a scream. Tristan freezes. What did he do? What crime has he committed?

I scrubbed, he thinks. Nothing more. Like for Mama, for Grandma.

Mrs. Klimt seizes the teapot, shakes it, caresses it, laments.

And then she calms down, almost just as suddenly, looks at him, touches his cheek. Her eyes are shining.

He remembers something the prefect said to him, about a son who died, or disappeared, or got angry about something. He doesn't know anymore. He feels that he's going to be very happy with Mrs. Klimt, that she'll take care of him like no one ever has before.

19

"So, you speak English?" interrupts Dumestre.

"Yes."

"That's neat, speaking another language. My parents spoke patois. The local dialect that's not too different from French. Except I can't speak it. Shit, it's raining."

"What should we do?"

"What do you think we should do?"

Heavy drops—mature, transparent fruit from the steel-colored sky—beat down on their foreheads, their cheeks, the backs of their hands.

"We could..."

"Continue the story. We'll be soaked one way or another. We'll tell the firemen to give us new clothes."

Dumestre sniggers, turns his head to one side, exposing the dry part of his face to the shower of nails, daggers, sabers.

20

The language school is a few steps from the Highbury and Islington subway station exit. Tristan congratulates himself each day on the simple itinerary he's mastering to perfection. The first time, however, he'd had some difficulty finding it; he was expecting to see a building with a large sign on which he would recognize the English word "school."

Nothing of the sort.

The address written in his vade mecum corresponds to a two-story house, made of brick and stucco, narrow, squeezed like the shy head of a child in a crowd of adults. Just in front of it, on either side of the columned porch, two tiny garden squares overrun with nettles and wild blackberry bushes clash, in a mix of arrogance and shame, with the neighbors' gardens, which are filled with well-pruned rosebushes, blooming nasturtium, exuberant dahlias, and wild asters.

Tristan is the sole pupil of Hector, a slender man, thin and round-shouldered, whose remarkably prominent

Adam's apple seems endowed with an autonomous existence. Hector serves Tristan black tea, bitter and heavy, and speaks for hours and hours, showing him photos of war ships, tanks, submarines. Sometimes he makes Tristan jot down a word in the notebook he provided for him: yellow pages with a small margin on the right and purple horizontal lines, not like the graph paper Tristan was used to using in France.

Everything is different here, thinks Tristan, thrilled and disconcerted; his solitude deepens with each new exoticism: the color of cookies, the shape of cups, the size of spoons, the chocolate wrappers, the glass milk bottles. It's as if he has to relearn everything.

Initially, he doesn't try to understand or translate the words Hector pronounces, which aren't really words but garlands—indivisible, twisted, undulating, turbulent, without beginning or end. Tristan tries above all else to convince his body that the new shapes around him must become as familiar as the ones he left behind.

After a few weeks, however, without his mind making any effort at deciphering them, he realizes that the stream of sounds has transformed into a torrent of words. He surprises himself by nodding his head and murmuring, without premeditation, a "Hmm, nice!" when shown a picture of a destroyer.

Classes take place in the morning. Afternoons are free. No one told him how he was supposed to spend them. On the first day, he went back to Mrs. Klimt's at lunchtime. The door was closed and she hadn't left him a key. He guessed she had gone out. She'd probably told him, explaining in her feathered gibberish—fluttering, scattered with delicate consonants; hissing, lisping, as though rimmed with air—that he should come back in the late afternoon. He hadn't understood. He hadn't heard. He was forced to make it up.

In front of the closed door, he tried to detect a sort of logic, thought about working hours, school schedules. She expects him, surely, for dinner.

When he returned the second time, after taking the bus all the way to the last stop in one direction, then the other, he found a distraught Mrs. Klimt on the front steps, her hair disheveled, her cheeks redder than the day before. He discerned the word "police" in the breathless sentences she was uttering while trying in spite of everything to smile at him, relieved. He concluded from this that people in England eat dinner earlier than in France. Seven P.M. wasn't the limit, the end of the day, the beginning of the evening. For Mrs. Klimt, seven was nighttime, danger, table cleared, dishes done, curfew.

The next day, he gambled on four P.M., judging that the fear his hostess had felt—hadn't she called the police?— signified he had been considerably late.

At four, door locked. Tristan sat down on the front steps. Fearing he'd be taken for a vagabond, he quickly got back up and began a tour around the block: to the left, first left, and to the left again, he knew how to not get lost in a foreign town. However, the streets of Seven Sisters (but maybe this was also the case elsewhere in London) didn't allow him to employ this tactic. Like the English language, English streets snaked and curved. The urban geometry in which he'd grown up was no help to him here. He got lost. Returning at 5:30, he found Mrs. Klimt angry but calm.

Five. Five in the afternoon. "Tea time," as she called it. For afternoon tea, you drank black tea with milk while savoring a meat pie and steamed vegetables in multiple colors that all had the same taste.

"NEVER!"

He recognized the word thanks to a song he used to listen to.

"Never!" Mrs. Klimt said to him, once the meal had ended, pointing to the interior of the teapot with her left index finger, deformed by arthritis, while shaking the scrub brush with her right hand.

"Never," said Tristan, nodding, before placing his hand on his heart. He solemnly swore never to clean the interior of the teapot again. If that was the wager, the secret, the open sesame of their shared life, he was entirely ready to yield to it.

"Never!" they cried together. It was the first time he'd burst out laughing in a long while.

Upon leaving Hector's, he eats an apple and a slice of extraordinarily soft and supple white bread for lunch. Then he roams the city by bus or on the subway, which the English call "the Tube." That's his routine. The repetition of the same. The stammer of days that all resemble one another gives him relief and rest from the persistent pain of exile. He watches people, trying to penetrate some mystery, but without clearly identifying which one. It's somewhat as if he were investigating a murder case without knowing anything about the crime: the number of victims, the place, the date, the time. Focused and tense, he perceives a sort of danger, but, not knowing where to start, he collects the evidence haphazardly, without any hierarchal order: the girls' tights are thick and full of holes; the men have very long eyebrows; the shoes seem comfortable (numerous black rubber soles); the pants are sometimes a little short; wearing suits is common, even for children; often, on public transportation, the passengers snack on chocolate bars or potato chips.

One afternoon, a young woman attracts his gaze: she has huge white cheeks crowned with pink cheekbones, small dark brown eyes set deeply and close together in her wide face, and two braids of fine red hair falling down onto her shoulders. She entered at the Elephant and Castle station and sat down facing him, ankles crossed, her skirt riding up on her fat white thighs, which are spread out on the velour of the seat. Her fingers, plump but long and thin at the ends, rummage around in a bag and rise very slowly to her fleshy pale pink mouth to insert, with the greatest care, a potato chip. She hardly moves her jaw, as if refusing to make a crunching noise. Tristan thinks of holy wafers, of sacrilege. He watches her; she is always slow, always careful, her hands similar to those of the Virgin of Quattrocento—long and pudgy. She is patient and calm, as if the tiny bag between her thighs were inexhaustible, bottomless, endless. He gets an erection. He blushes.

21

This isn't exactly how Tristan tells his story to Dumestre. He doesn't tell him everything. He doesn't use words like "stammer" or "arrogance." He sticks to the facts, which he has to shout because of the wind carrying away his words, the thunder rumbling, the rain hammering down.

The two men have decided to defy the storm. Fresh streams of water slip under their collars; their legs are already soaked. Their feet are protected by shoes, their chests by the double thickness of a sweater and a jacket, but not for long. Soon, they'll be swimming in the deceptive warmth of a thin layer of water circulating between their skin and clothing. Deceptive, because it's ephemeral. The warmth won't last. The nice slime will quickly become ice cold from the wind and their immobility.

This, thinks the rabbit, is a very serious problem. It's your species' main weakness. I don't understand how you could have rid yourselves of your body hair. Was it out of vanity at first? Were you so anxious to distinguish yourselves from us that you agreed to give up your fleece?

But maybe you didn't choose. Maybe you're undergoing a natural degeneration. You didn't decide anything. Under your efficient exteriors, your domineering exteriors, you don't decide anything. Someone is playing with you, someone is fooling you, but who? Who could be so cruel, so mischievous, so fiendish, as to deprive you of the best thermoregulation system there is?

Take the word for "fur" in French. *Pelage.* The word itself is soft. And for what reason do you think you can hear in it, like an echo, like its root, the French word *peau*, for skin? Precisely because hair is born in skin, planting itself there so tightly that water can't get through, but not so much that air can't get through. This way, our skin breathes without fear of getting wet.

It's already starting to smell like carrion in your clothes—they're not permeable enough to let your pores exhale, yet too permeable to prevent water from enveloping you. Your stench is astounding. Never smelled anything like it. If I were you, I'd dig a hole—yes, I know, whatever the situation, I'll always propose a hole as the solution, but listen for a moment: you dig a hole and undress yourselves, then you shove your clothes into the hole so they stay dry. You run and you jump to warm yourselves up. Your skin breathes, you're clean, and when the rain stops, you just have to dry yourselves in the sun, or the wind, or simply the air, and put your clothes back on. That way you'll be warm. That way you'll be covered up. Because, yes, I know it's very important for you to be covered up. Just what is your problem with nudity, anyway?

Nudity, thinks Tristan. Nudity... But it's not easy to think while speaking, while enduring the assaults of a storm. So words burst out one at a time, like on the surface of a volcanic mud pool: "nudity," "shame," "fear," "sexuality."

Oh yes, goes the rabbit. Sex. Sex is a very important thing for you humans.

It's important for everyone, Tristan counterattacks. It's important for animals, and especially for you rabbits. He almost starts laughing. A rabbit asking about sex, would you look at that.

We don't call that sex, replies the rabbit, we talk about reproduction, and, personally, I regard those two notions as having nothing to do with each other.

You damn papist, says Tristan, outraged.

It takes one to know one, retorts the rabbit. Then just as quickly, he moves on: I heard this story, I can't remember where, can't remember when: "They knew that they were naked." Everything started from there, after all, from your lack of fur. Take us, for example, we're never naked. Let me start again. You exhibited your naked skin, and that, it seems, caused your kind lots of problems, problems with desire. You became obscene; you became indecent. You knew shame and lustfulness. That's sex. Where I come from, there aren't so many problems. We kept our fur; we have our hearts set on reproducing, by instinct, because you hunt us, because you—not just you humans, of course, but also foxes and other creatures, let's be fair—you decimate us. We don't have the choice, we don't ask ourselves questions, we fuck to survive, that's called perpetuating the species. But you, you live to fuck, that's called sex. They're two completely distinct activities, I assure you. I understand. It's so complicated for you humans, whereas for animals, it's functional. Certain fish are born female, then become male, because it's practical, and for no other reason. And...

Tristan gently presses his thumb on the rabbit's muzzle. He's had enough. He wants to continue his story. He has to distract Dumestre. He tells the story because he's endowed with speech, true speech, and intelligence as well, real intelligence. He speaks, rather than dancing naked in the rain, because he hasn't spent millions of years evolving with persistence and tenacity in order to behave like an animal.

"And you didn't find that strange, you and this teacher, all alone in his pad? Where'd this guy come from? I wouldn't have trusted him. I mean, shit, school isn't just for show, it's more than just some perv showing warships to a defenseless kid."

Dumestre didn't appreciate the chapter about Hector. He thinks it's shady.

"And that still doesn't explain how your mother died either. Oh, shit, I feel the cold coming up my stomach."

"And your feet?"

"Don't talk to me about my feet, understand? Finish your fucking story and then we'll see. I thought I heard a siren. Didn't you hear a siren?"

"Yes," Tristan admits, without adding that it was far away and had seemed to get even farther before disappearing in the ambient racket.

The light has suddenly grown so dim that it looks like dusk. But it's the middle of the afternoon. Almost tea time. They won't be drinking any tea, nor any of that marvelous coffee with the taste of scrap metal they'd enjoyed a few hours ago.

"Peretti could've left us his thermos, at least," Dumestre grumbles.

"At this point, we would've been better off with Farnèse's plonk," answers Tristan in an awkward attempt at manly fraternization.

The mere act of uttering the word "plonk" makes Tristan uneasy. He would also rather refer to their alcoholic hunting companion by his first name, but he doesn't know what it is. When people don't call him Farnèse, they call him Titi. Titi for Thierry, probably. But if no one says Thierry, then... then...

"Don't make fun of Farnèse," says Dumestre after a moment. "He's an unlucky guy. Before, he was sharp. He worked as a roofer. The love of a job well done, that's what he had. Gotta have lots of balance in that job, lots of composure. They called Farnèse 'the Tightrope Walker.' He used to skip across rooftops, never wearing a harness, even for a church restoration that went up some fifty or sixty feet. Never wore a hard hat. Just a strange pair of diving fins, totally unorthodox. You know what I mean. No one in the trade wears anything like it. Those guys wear heavy boots. And him—that's how you know he's a character—he does it in rubber flippers. Speaking of which, this word, 'unorthodox'—like something from Greek or Chinese—it's his word. He'd say: 'Might be unorthodox, but it works!'

"He had a thing with the school principal when he was still just a kid. The principal, would you believe it? Not a teacher. The principal herself, who was gorgeous. He must've been about eighteen. The principal wasn't old, maybe in her thirties. Still, it was impossible love, you know? He was working as an apprentice with Lamalle, the roofer, but he had this taste for the finer things. Who knows where quirks like that come from? Like poppies at the edges of wheat fields. A seed must've been carried by the wind and planted in his head. For example, you put a musical instrument in his hands—any kind, right?—and he makes it sing for you. So of course, we call him 'the Gypsy.' Tightrope Walker at work, the Gypsy at the café.

"He used to love complicated words too, like 'unorthodox.' I don't remember the other ones. The principal didn't really give a damn about it, she knew more complicated words than he did. What she was looking for was adventure. She was a beautiful woman, but a sad one, and that's a terrible thing. A sad woman, that's something that shouldn't exist. It's the most dangerous thing for a man. Shit, my teeth are chattering. What's the temperature you freeze to death?"

"I don't know," goes Tristan, dumbfounded. (He had gotten caught up in Farnèse's romantic tragedy and forgotten the rain, the cold, the thunder.) "I don't know," he says again, "but I do know we're going to get through this. I'm going to dig a hole."

"We just got out of a fucking hole!" Dumestre growls.

"A different hole. Like a burrow. Really solid, one that won't cave in on us. The temperature is consistent underground. With that, plus our body heat, we'll surely be able to withstand this better. We can even spend the night in there if we have to."

He gets to work immediately. Since the earth resists him, he cuts into the crust with the butt of his rifle.

"I hope that's not loaded," says Dumestre.

Tristan checks, takes out the cartridges, wipes the cold sweat running along his temples.

He almost put a bullet in his head.

He starts up again, with the butt of the rifle, with the barrel, his hands, his feet. He's surprised he knows what to do, performing the motions with such precision. Surprised he's not panicking, and even estimating the danger so precisely. He has realized that this isn't an ordinary storm. What's beating down on them, what's about to come down hard on them, is something else. It's what insurance policies designate a "natural disaster." But the more adequate term would be "supernatural disaster," because in a few hours, nothing will be recognizable anymore. The heights will have joined the depths, the depths will replace the heights. Tristan doesn't have the least experience with an event like this, but it's as if some disposition within him, dormant until now, has suddenly awoken, picked up the vibrations, the undulations, the rattling, the rolling, the slamming, the grating. The more his hands feel the earth, the more they're learning about the nature of what's going to sweep over them.

The skepticism that systematically keeps him from picturing the improbable doesn't intervene. It's not a question of plausibility, it's certain: in a few hours, but maybe less—maybe it's nothing but a few minutes—chaos will get the upper hand. Freed from who knows where, it will extend its monstrous hand, deft at kneading the earth with no regard for its inhabitants.

Emma.

Emma, alone in their house.

He forgot about her. He abandoned her. His wife. His wife who wants him to join the men, to fit in; his wife who sent him hunting. He agreed. She knew. Emma is like the ancient peoples. She has an innate sense of savagery.

He doesn't understand why he's suddenly so annoyed with her. As if she betrayed him, as if she sent him to his death. Yet she's the one who's in danger, in their poorly insulated house, with its pointed roof, flood prone, perhaps already flooded. Inside him, like outside, a storm is brewing. A voice that has long kept quiet rises up and growls. They're not connected anymore, not united as two against the world; they're trained on each other in opposing combat. Her will against his. Her idea against his. Their love has gone wrong. Their love has turned into a business deal, a millstone to grind away the days. Their consideration for each other suddenly disgusts him, this polite rubbing of shoulders, this reasonable effort so their business can function, so they can fit in, become like the others.

What is a female for, where you come from? asks the rabbit. Why don't you have children?

Tristan refuses to hear this question, refuses to continue these crazy thoughts, these doubts inspired by fear. He must dig. He digs. Like a maniac. When he's already waist-high in the earth, warmed up by the effort, he slips out of the burrow to give Dumestre his jacket.

Poking his head out of the hole, he catches sight of his companion, who, unaware he's being observed, bends one knee, then the other, in order to reawaken his legs. Instead of rejoicing and congratulating Dumestre on the return of his mobility, Tristan crawls back underground and calls out to his comrade from the bottom of the burrow: "Do you want my jacket? I'm burning up down here."

He pulls himself out for the second time and discovers Dumestre, his legs out and motionless, propped up on his elbows to get closer.

"Looks like your arms are better," risks Tristan. "And your legs, still nothing?"

"You want me to draw you a picture or what? I have a broken spinal column, isn't that clear? You think the Holy Spirit's just going to bless me with some miracle?"

"Sorry," says Tristan.

He clambers over to Dumestre and drapes his jacket over his companion's large chest.

"Your coat's soaked," grumbles the cripple.

"It'll still protect you a little," says Tristan, tucking in Dumestre's immobile body as best he can. Then he takes off his sweater and puts it around the thick neck like a scarf. "I'm making headway. Don't worry."

His hands are trembling. Is it because of fatigue, hunger, thirst? Is it because of fear? He isn't equipped to deal with dishonesty, never has been. Like something vital is missing.

22

The usual. The everyday. The new life chases away the old life. Sometimes Tristan forgets that he hasn't always lived in London, that he wasn't born in Seven Sisters. He pronounces the two syllables of "ma-*ma*" in his head the French way, with the stress on the second syllable. He's become so used to her death that it's almost as if she never existed. And in these moments, these moments when he remembers who he was and what he went through, he is overcome with a sense of grief deeper than loss. The loss of loss, that's what threatens him. An immaterial grief, boundless, with infinite dominion.

English comes into his mouth, settles down in his palate, behind his teeth, on the tip of his tongue. His voice changes, the muscles in his cheeks and lips reorganize themselves around this new nucleus. His jaw learns to loosen, slacken, yield, allowing the vertical vowels of the learned language to stay up, to occupy all the available space from his nose to his chin. A new soft palate forms, a palate like a sail swelled up with the wind of the aspirated "h." Although "aspirated" is the official term, it actually comes from exhalation. "HER," he pronounces: a long, uniform vowel, standing at attention, no diphthong to be found, preceded by the billowing of his palatal jib sail. Sometimes he even has the impression that his face and body are changing as a result of this learning process. English has penetrated him, and now Tristan feels liberated from his old shell. His voice is different. He's being reborn.

Mrs. Klimt announces a surprise. A visit. He's going to be "extremely happy." She squeezes him in her arms and pats him on the back. Tristan is currently mastering the choreography of the hug, so different and nevertheless equivalent to that of the French *bise*—the kiss. He has often wanted to kiss both of Mrs. Klimt's rosy cheeks, but he knows it's forbidden, as forbidden as cleaning the teapot. In England, you don't embrace with the mouth, you embrace in the real sense of the word: you entwine, you take the other person's body in your arms, you pat their back. The face has no part in it; it remains inactive, over the partner's shoulder. At first, like a reflex, Tristan's lips tried to plant themselves somewhere, but he quickly realized. The awkwardness he created in the beginning with his French mouth, which was absolutely set on smacking a kiss, had been sufficiently painful. This seems ridiculous to him now, as if he'd asked to suck on the person's face.

He has no idea who is coming to visit him. He doesn't know anyone. Mrs. Klimt alluded to the extreme happiness the meeting would lavish on him. Tristan can't think of who would be in a position to provide him with such a thing. "Extremely happy." He never has been, or then again, yes, as a child, in the beginning. Mama, naked, running on the beach; Mama running naked with her childlike body, not a strange, revolting body like those of other mamas. His own mama is very small, very thin, very wiry, very tan. She looks like Mowgli in *The Jungle Book*. She grabs Tristan by his feet and whirls him around. He flies. He extends his arms. Then he really flies. His mother has that kind of strength, the strength to make him fly.

On the specified day, the doorbell rings at six in the evening. Special meals are served later than five o'clock tea at Mrs. Klimt's. Tristan is in his bedroom, reading a novel Hector lent him: *Typhoon*. "This book," his teacher had explained, "was written in English by a man who didn't grow up speaking our language. Joseph Conrad learned English, like you're doing today, and became one of the greatest modern novelists. You can change the course of things, don't you see? In my opinion, territorial blessings and curses don't exist. The world belongs to us. Languages belong to us. We just have to take hold of them. They don't resist. For them, it's an honor to be had." Hector converses more and more to his student, always speaking slowly and articulating excessively to assure himself the boy understands. He isn't just satisfied with his pupil—he's blown away by the young man, by his curiosity, his gentleness, the emptiness inside him and around him. Hector had a son, in the past, with Mrs. Klimt, but no one ever talks about it, no one knows, Tristan remains unaware.

Typhoon is a difficult book. Tristan understands English, but he doesn't understand *Typhoon* yet. He's been struggling on the first page for three days. Mrs. Klimt calls him. Tristan reads the word "bashfulness," wonders what it means. He hears Mrs. Klimt pronounce his name with her lips that can't make the French nasal sound of "*an*." She says, "Tristam, you don't mind, do you?"

She calls him once more. He closes the book on the page he doesn't need to dog-ear, because it's always the same one.

At the bottom of the stairs, he sees an ankle and a high heel poised on the first step. This is the foot of the person who's going to bring me extreme happiness, he thinks.

23

The wind redoubles in force. The storm is unleashed. Rain had been forecasted, but no one expected this. Fire trucks go up and down the roads to sound the alarm. They start by evacuating the school. Children jump in puddles, get slapped, cry. Adults yell, push them, carry them. Someone shouts that the river has burst its banks. This makes them laugh. A river bursting the banks! Ha ha! They laugh and cry at the same time. The youngest ones call for their mommies. The mommies, in their houses, wring their hands, look out the window, turn on the radio. No more electricity. Night falls as if someone suddenly pulled a black curtain over the village. Cars lift up off the ground, wobble, gently swirl, then, like a docile herd being led to the slaughterhouse, move into the streets, tossed about by a torrent of mud, rumbling as it rolls along. Basement windows shatter under the pressure. Cellars fill with pebbles, water, earth, rubble, silt vomited by the river. The most adventurous residents—the brave, the crazy, the miserly—come out of their homes wearing fishing boots to save what they can.

The children are safe in the community center adjoining the town hall, located on higher ground. They are given stale cookies from last Christmas. They eat them. One of the teachers is crying. She says her baby is at his nanny's. The nanny lives in the old windmill, at the river's edge. The firefighters reassure her, explaining that this isn't going to last; they've evacuated the school as a precautionary measure, but everything is under control. She doesn't believe them. She races toward the door. She wants to go save her baby herself. The children cheer her on. Go, teacher! The teacher knows how to do everything. She knows how to swim. She is good at geography. She knows the names of all the rivers and all the streams in France, maybe even in the world. She knows how to make bumps disappear and how to put on Band-Aids that never come off. They trust her. But the firefighters grab her by the waist, scold her, tackle her to the ground. She doesn't have the right to go save her baby. The children throw themselves onto the firefighters. They want to save the teacher so she can go save her baby. They kick and bite. Go, teacher! They all know her baby. She brought him to class when he was born. His name is Nino. He is very small. He doesn't have any hair. He wears pajamas all day. Go, teacher! The other teacher, the one who has a grown son at reform school because he keeps stealing mopeds, grabs the children by their collars and sends them flying, all the while screaming that if they keep it up, they won't go to the forest, the pool, the fair; that they'll never see their mommies again. They don't listen to a thing. They're like the river. They're bursting their banks. Nothing will stop them, nothing will make them be quiet.

But then the nice teacher, Nino's mommy, who has escaped from the free-for-all, suddenly stands up in front of them and says: "It's okay, children, I'm going to tell a story now." She's not crying. She has regained her normal voice, her normal head. The children stop their assault, sit cross-legged, like she taught them to do, in order to really concentrate. A sweaty fireman with disheveled hair and scarlet cheeks offers her a chair. She sits down and puts her hand under her chin, like she always does when thinking of what story she's going to tell.

"What about Nino?" asks a small voice from the group at her feet.

"Nino is very strong," she says.

"Does he know how to swim?"

"Yes."

"How did he learn?"

"He learned in my stomach," she responds.

The children nod seriously. Of course, they say to themselves, that's normal. He's the teacher's son.

24

After the kicking of the tires, the mutual accusations—"It's your fault!" "And you couldn't have thought of it?"—the threats, the hands reassuring themselves on the butts of the rifles, Farnèse and Peretti have decided to be efficient. They call the fire department. But no one answers at the station.

"Firefighters never really give a fuck about anything. What a cushy job!" says Peretti.

"Maybe there was a fire," Farnèse remarks.

"Do you see smoke anywhere, stupid?"

"No, but I thought I heard a siren earlier."

"You and your sirens," says Peretti, chuckling. "To stop hearing them, you have to stop listening to 'em."

Farnèse doesn't take offense. He tilts his head to the side. Notices something. Doesn't mention it to his companion. Isn't sure what to do with it. Something is absent from the scenery. A piece is missing. Like a table leg, thinks Farnèse. A pillar without which the world would collapse. He thinks. Racks his brain. Knows he must absolutely not give anything away. The scenery, yes, that's it, except it's not a visual concern. Nothing is lacking from the landscape. Everything is in its place. The problem is the sound. No birdsong. Nothing. No chattering, no chirping, no cawing. Reassured to have discovered it, but worried by his discovery, Farnèse sets off, with Peretti on his heels. They calculate that by walking at a good pace, they'll reach the village in less than an hour.

Farnèse scampers along, hops. He doesn't know how to walk, so he inevitably starts running, he can't help it. Peretti struggles to keep up, remembering the time when they used to call him the Tightrope Walker, with his funny diving flippers. He also remembers something else. It's like a shadow, a border. He doesn't want this memory, but it's stubborn, it comes back, clings to Farnèse's bounding silhouette. The Tightrope Walker was never alone. Beside him, stuck to him, right there, clinging to his pants, was the child.

The child's name was Vladimir, but Peretti doesn't want to remember that either. Or how they had teased Farnèse because of that name. Another one of the principal's ideas, they'd said. They had all been wary of this woman. All of them, his friends. And they had been right. As soon as the kid was born, she disappeared—no news, no address, no heart in fact.

Vladimir and his father had resembled each other, like two apples from the same tree. Same light feet, same clever smile, pointed nose, pale blue eyes always wide open. Farnèse kissed him all the time, carried him on his back, on his shoulders, in his arms. One time, they called him "the Kangaroo," but it didn't stick. Tightrope Walker, Gypsy, that was enough.

"May he who has ever changed Vladimir's diaper cast the first stone!" That was the type of joke they had loved to make among themselves, because Farnèse was the only one with a child at the time and they had all helped him as much as they could. Oddly, their girlfriends weren't interested. Vladimir was a born mascot. Voilà. Vladimir wasn't a child, he was a mascot. And girlfriends didn't understand this, but for men, a mascot is better than a child.

Peretti watches his companion, who's really limping more than running because his muscles have melted from drinking so much, and he can't help picturing a miniature Farnèse alongside. Except the mascot doesn't run anymore. The mascot fell off a roof. And it wasn't Farnèse's fault. It was that witch's fault, that bitch, that fucking principal. If she hadn't come back, Vladimir would still be there, would have become a man, with his own little boy with a funny name, or a little girl with pigtails and a Spanish dress. But the principal came back. She wanted to see him. She saw him. Farnèse said to Vladimir, "Uh, well, this is your mother." And the next day, Vladimir fell off the roof.

"A child doesn't just fall," Lamalle, the boss, kept repeating. He had been charged because the roof was his responsibility. "In the old days, I'd take my apprentices at thirteen, fourteen years old and they'd never fall. It's the old ones who fall, because of dizzy spells, because of being fed up, but children, never. You fall if you think about it. Children don't think about it."

It seems that on that day, Vladimir had thought about it.

"C'mon, hurry up," says Farnèse, turning around. "Look what's over our heads."

He points to the sky. Peretti sees the enormous cloud, like a roll of steel wool ready to beat down on them. He doesn't recognize the sky. He's never seen anything like it.

"What is that?" he asks Farnèse.

Farnèse shrugs his shoulders. The rain starts to fall, very hard, all at once, as if to answer the question. The drops almost hurt, they're so heavy. It feels like they're loaded with lead.

After Vladimir died, Farnèse often had a nightmare in which he was lying on the ground, watching the sky, and could perceive millions and millions of eyeballs hanging over him. Today, it's as though all those eyes were falling, and without actually thinking about it, without really making the connection, he's delighted, in his own way, very modestly.

The end of the world, he thinks. Phew, it's about time.

25

The two men have settled into their cave. Tristan pulled Dumestre along the tunnel, then to the bottom of the hole he had widened in order to build a cave. Outside, night has fallen. Inside, the darkness is so black, so thick, it seems material. The absence of light has transformed into cotton wool. At first, the eyes strain, searching for a hint of brightness, waiting for the moment when the pupil has sufficiently dilated and the optic nerve can send new information to the brain: no, it's not completely black. A feeling from childhood. Awoken from a dream, from a nightmare, you open your blind eyes. Where are you? Where did the room go? Where has the world gone? But the iris retracts and the scenery is repainted with the gray paintbrush of the moon, the yellow paintbrush of the streetlight on the corner, the red paintbrush of the flickering sign. The night is filled with colors.

Tristan flicks on his lighter, makes his companion admire the walls. Even he can't get over the work he accomplished. Alone, with his bare hands. He never would have thought he possessed such strength.

Inside, they can't hear the rain or the wind. Once the lighter goes out, nothing is visible. The eye bumps into what's called blackness, but it's no more black than it is green or blue. The eye is dismissed; it has no more sensitivity than the back of a hand, the crook of an elbow—it can see no more than the rest of the body does. The earth's odor mixes with that of sweat. Tristan has convinced Dumestre to take his clothes off. "They'll dry quicker if they aren't on us," he told him.

"Don't you touch my underwear!" Dumestre orders after letting himself be undressed.

"No, no, of course not. Don't worry. I'm keeping my boxers on too."

Tristan sorts the clothes by touch, spreading them out as much as possible. The sweaters aren't as wet as the rest. The two men slip them back on, bumping into the walls, bumping into each other. They grumble. They laugh.

"Shit, if somebody had told me," mumbles Dumestre, "if somebody'd told me..."

Tristan flicks on his lighter again, an orange globe making their faces come alive in the darkness.

He turns it off once more.

"You know 'The Little Match Girl'?" he asks.

"What's that?" asks Dumestre. "A song?"

"No, a story."

"Let's hear it."

So, as slowly as possible, Tristan tells the Hans Christian Andersen tale, which he can't remember very well. It's a trick. A trick to distract Dumestre from the other story, the one he started telling in the rain but can't continue there, alone with him, almost naked, at the bottom of a hole.

26

"Extremely happy," Tristan repeats to himself, all while evoking the extremely sad adventures of the little match girl.

A little girl, on a winter evening, without shoes, walks in the snow.

A teenaged girl, wearing high heels, sets an enticing foot on the first step of a London staircase.

And so, like a game of point and counterpoint, the stories respond to each other and superimpose.

This is the foot of the person who's going to bring me extreme happiness, Tristan thinks, sixteen and a half years old, coming down the stairs to meet his surprise.

The ankle is at once dainty and plump, a slender joint and ample flesh, fattened with who knows what, ripe, as though ready to burst. The skin sparkles between the bottom of the pant leg and the shoe's leather.

From the back, he doesn't recognize her.

Alerted by the noise, by Mrs. Klimt's joyful cries, the visitor turns around.

From the front, he doesn't recognize her either.

She seems older than he is, but barely. The skin on her face is greasy, as if she has just finished coating it with butter. Little red pimples border her hairline like a diadem. She wears her hair short, like a boy's. Her cheeks are round, her eyes sad and brown with deep purple rings under them, her mouth painted a brick red that aggravates her skin's brownish tint.

"You recognize me?" she asks in a husky, powerful, authoritative voice.

Without wanting to, Tristan lowers his eyes slightly toward her chest. Her open jacket and blouse reveal two perfect breasts. That's how he describes them to himself, his crotch aching, before thinking, What a treat.

"Astre," he says.

"Yeah," she responds.

What happened to her kilt? he thinks. And her ballet bun? Where are her skinny legs, her gaunt torso, her slumped shoulders?

Mrs. Klimt is over the moon.

Tristan wonders if he's changed too. He quickly glances at his reflection in the mirror hanging in the lounge. He sees his enormous hands, much too big for his bony arms; his eyebrows, probably thicker than they were ten years ago; his mouth that droops a little, always half-open, except when he thinks about it and abruptly closes it again, clenching his jaw until the roots of his teeth hurt. His hair is longer than Astre's.

Yes, I've changed too, he thinks, trying with one hand, which has slid into his pants pocket, to crush his swelling penis, taking up all the space and threatening to tear the fabric of his jeans, to break everything in sight...

Tristan smiles. He realizes he's funny. He realizes he's joyful. Extremely happy.

Astre is funny too.

She eats everything Mrs. Klimt gives her with a voracious appetite, and, looking at the woman gratefully, with her hand on her heart, she says in French, "This is super disgusting, it's dog food, right?"

And Mrs. Klimt, who doesn't understand a word, nods, saying, "Yes, *oui, oui.*"

Tristan is a little embarrassed to be laughing at the expense of his hostess, but it's irresistible. He has never known someone as intrepid, as crazy as this girl.

As for Astre, she doesn't laugh, but manages to keep a straight face and preserve her aristocratic manners, which, Tristan notices, have made a big impression on Mrs. Klimt.

"Charming girl! Charming girl!" she confides to her protégé in a low voice, her eyes closed, her hands joined, as if Astre isn't listening, isn't there.

After the meal, Mrs. Klimt refuses to let the kids clear up or do the dishes. She has a better idea. She sits them down in the lounge with a game of Monopoly. Do they know how to play Monopoly?

"Of course we know how, you old hag!" Astre says in French in a very sweet voice, showing signs of acknowledgment. "You can go scrape the shit off your dishes."

Mrs. Klimt brings them a plate of cookies. The two teenagers don't exchange a word. They play. Roll the dice. Buy properties. Go to jail. Get out of it. Tristan is winning. He becomes a billionaire. Astre sinks into mediocrity, then misery. They don't exchange glances either. They play. Tristan grabs his partner's last paper bills.

"Well, I'm going to bed," she barks, knocking over the game board by accident—a very purposeful accident. "Oh, sorry. Can you clean it up? I'm exhausted."

Tristan feels like he missed something. He should have... He could have... He probably did something wrong, but what? He picks up the scattered cards and pieces with trembling hands. His breath is short, uneven, as though he has a fever.

I screwed everything up, he thinks, without really knowing what "everything" is. What was he expecting? Should he have let her win? Should he have said something special to her, looked at her in a certain way, in certain places?

The house is immersed in silence. It's the eight o'clock curfew.

Tristan doesn't know where Astre's room is. He knows she's going to sleep here tonight. He can almost feel her, on his skin, in his throat, on his palms, due to a particular feeling of idleness, a sense of boredom, a weariness that takes hold of certain areas of his body.

He returns to his book, right where he left off, on the first page, the insurmountable first page, which he goes beyond this time, without effort, without understanding anything else, drifting on the surface of the sentences, compelled by an anger he doesn't know how to handle, his thighs clenched, as he lies on his ridiculous bed, a pitiful skiff. He reads, turns the pages, going forward as though rowing, producing a mechanical effort, his gaze absent, his ear straining, listening for the noise of footsteps, creaking doors, water running from a faucet, and—much fainter, almost imperceptible, imaginary, in fact—a duvet falling on the tawny skin of a body in bloom.

He distracts himself from reading, to the point of nausea. Yet without the help of his sight and hearing, absorbed as they are by the most urgent missions, something in him, something childish or, on the contrary, something old and wise, accepts the reading, soaks it up, thrives on it, gets lost in it, becomes enamored with it. He recognizes himself in Captain MacWhirr, this man who doesn't understand anything at all, unshakable because of his slowness, because of his stupidity, but most of all because of something more secret and complicated, a hidden factor that Tristan feels he alone can detect. MacWhirr is always wrong and always right at the same time; when he says to Jukes, his second-in-command, *Was that you talking just now in the port alley-way? With the third engineer? I can't understand what you can find to talk about. Two solid hours,* Tristan feels a deep sense of recognition. He doesn't understand conversation either. He feels both full and empty. Full of feelings and empty of words. He lacks a point of access, which he sometimes pictures as a footbridge, but other times as the near-invisible thread of a spider's web. Is this link supposed to stretch between thoughts and words, or between him and others? Tristan doesn't know. Where can this missing link be found—inside or outside of himself?

His eyes close on this question, on the disturbingly strong forces rocking the *Nan-Shan*, this ship, *le navire* in French—but in English, you call a ship "she," or *la navire*, and it's so much prettier, so much nobler than the masculine version in French, Tristan says to himself, captivated by the language that is adopting him as much as he's adopting it—this ship that, thanks to the stubbornness of

MacWhirr, *her* idiot captain, is rushing right into the ty-phoon.

A light being turned off wakes him up for one second. Someone has slipped into his room. Someone has closed his book and set it on the nightstand. Someone has pressed the little black button at the base of the lightbulb. Some-one who wants the best for him, who's taking care of him, who's watching over him. So he quickly sinks into a deeper, rapid sleep, inhaled as if through a siphon by the absence of conscience, the absence of light, the absence of self.

He is still sleeping, with belligerence and passion, when a hand places itself on his hip bone. A crystal laugh as light as pollen opens up a passage in his dream. The hand on his iliac bone is the wave against the ship's side, *her* side, this hermaphrodite vessel, masculine or feminine as it passes from one native tongue to the other.

A real tongue slips into his mouth, between his lips, which are wide open. It's a sturdy tongue, long and will-ful, which Tristan thinks is his, but no, his own tongue is asleep, curled up in his lower jaw. A hand slides onto the hollow of his stomach, following the slope of his skinny torso, the pointed bone springing up from the vulnerable, resting loins. A hand, a tongue, and, soon, another hand busying itself, in a frenzy, much more agitated, much more nervous than the first. The second hand is a squir-rel; Tristan's body, a trunk. The squirrel scampers about, climbs up, climbs down, digs around, nestles, scurries away. Tristan's hands are still sleeping. Clumsy, ignorant paws. Tristan's hands don't know what they're missing. They still belong, despite their size, despite the instinct propelling them toward his groin, to childhood. They are the last to be contaminated, poisoned, intoxicated. Strange knees and incredible thighs, so fleshy, so smooth and round, substitute themselves for his. Tristan becomes *le/la navire*. The swell makes him swing from masculine to feminine; a strange slime, a complete wetness, covers his skin, drowns him, swallows him up. His fingers brush the sheet, pull up the already-wrinkled cotton of a nightshirt, lift up an underskirt, a wave of imaginary underskirts, white foam, frothy and clammy. His tongue wakes up, called in by his hands for reinforcement: lick here, suck there. The whole crew is on deck, battling against the unrelenting waves, fastening, rowing, hauling. They all come up in order to dive further into the deep, the wet, the sea that no longer knows high or low, over or under. Tristan groans and fights the hydra with its multiple heads and innumerable tentacles, his fists pounding and plowing, his fingers separating and digging in and grabbing on. He's bitten; he bites. He's pleaded with; he pleads. He's torn apart; he gives way; he consents. Don't scream, don't scream, don't scream. As long as this stops. As long as this never stops.

That laugh again.

"Well, there you go," says Astre in her husky voice that makes the walls shudder. "A job well done."

Tristan wants to stroke her face, as if to assure himself it's really her, it's really him, they're really here, but she pushes his hand away forcefully.

"Stop," she scolds. "I can't stand sentimentalism. It's disgusting. You and your family are such losers."

What family? Tristan wonders, without daring to open his mouth.

"Like your mother, completely ridiculous. Even when I was little, I felt sorry for her. She was so full of herself. My father called her 'Love'—wait, no, not my father, it was my uncle, the prefect. Love! She's probably the one who invented that nickname. Who did she think she was? A rebel? What was her rebellion, sleeping around? Shooting up? Drinking? All three? Frankly, they all pretty much lead to self-destruction. But dying from AIDS, on top of everything else. Such a loser."

Tristan feels his jaw tense up, his fists clench, his arm muscles contract.

"From AIDS?" he murmurs, even though he wants to scream at his cousin—but is she really his cousin if she's the prefect's niece?—to make her shut up. Even though he'd like to strangle her, slap her, gouge her eyes out.

"Don't you know about AIDS? The disease for junkies, gays, and sluts like your mother?"

Tristan doesn't answer.

"Well, wanna do it again?" she asks, indifferent.

And so they do it again, any way she says, upside down, right side up. It's a lesson, an express Kama Sutra, a trip around the world in eighty minutes.

27

"My mother died of AIDS," says Tristan, like an epilogue to "The Little Match Girl."

Dumestre mutters. He yawns. "Shit, I fell asleep. How does it end?"

"She dies."

"I thought so," Dumestre says. "It couldn't have ended any other way. What about us?"

"What?"

"You think we're gonna die?"

"What do you want us to die from?"

"Dunno. I'm hungry. Just think, if the partridge hadn't got left in that hole, we could've had one hell of a roast."

"The partridge?" asks Tristan, dazed.

He's lost the thread of the conversation. The word Dumestre didn't hear and will never hear still resounds in his own head: AIDS, like a single wobbling music note. My mother died of AIDS. He had never uttered that sentence before. He'd never had the chance. Even with Emma. When they were getting to know each other, it was too early, they were too young, and then, in the passing years, it had become too late.

"The partridge I wanted to give you for your wife. Remember it? Pretty little thing."

A pretty little thing, Tristan thinks. And, for a moment, he's no longer sure if this epithet applies to the bird or to Emma.

He's hungry too. He thinks of the rabbit. The rabbit in the gamebag. What have I done with him? he wonders.

Because of fear, because of the storm, he forgot his promise, he neglected his duty.

"I think I left my bag outside," he says to Dumestre in an anxious voice.

"What's in there? A bar of gold?"

"No, nothing, but, well, it's bad form."

This sentence that makes no sense seems to satisfy Dumestre; he nods in the darkness.

"Go ahead," he says. "Go find it. That way you can take a look around, see if the rescuers are coming."

Tristan crawls along the narrow tunnel and, as he approaches the entrance, he perceives the racket, louder and louder, more and more worrying, that prevails outside their burrow. Rolling, rumbling, grinding, wrenching. His eyes, accustomed to the half-light, distinguish the smallest details of the nocturnal spectacle that together are offering up the heavens and the earth.

Anger, rage. Everything is possible: the earth can open up; it can shake, cave in, swallow things. It's like some monster, after sleeping under the earth's crust for millennia, has awoken from its long hibernation. It stretches its colossal limbs, its joints unfold, its thick skin unfurls, it howls, it yawns, arches its back and sets forth, breaking the horizon line, smashing ridges, trampling valleys.

Tristan no longer knows if it's hot or cold outside. He feels swept up by a movement that surpasses him. His body is nothing. His thoughts collide with what he sees, without understanding it.

A pale yellow stroke slices the heavenly canopy. The clouds, which have lost their immateriality, as though loaded with iron filings, with soil, with pebbles, race toward either side of the bright arc. A cow moos, then wails, as if to announce the clap of thunder that flashes moments later, making the ground tremble. Trees several feet tall bend under the wind's hand, making them look as flexible as strands of hair. Sparkles glisten all around. That's water, thinks Tristan. Water in the place where, a few hours ago, there was a field.

Farther away, a little lower down, through the rain's dense, silvery strokes, he notices a shape that's difficult to identify, moving about majestically. What is that? he wonders, studying the triangle—yes, it's definitely a triangle—sliding along the valley, slowly, lazily, apparently inhabited with a different tempo. That house, Tristan says to himself, but the word "house" resists, doesn't identify with this moving shape; so he tries "barn," and the sentence manages to build itself: that barn is floating on the prairie.

It's not over, he says to himself. It's right in the middle of happening. A storm. A rise in water level. A flood. We're not going to die. Dumestre and I are already survivors. Nothing can happen to us here, where we are. But the others, in the village... Tristan hoists himself out of the hole to look for any lights. A wave of mud, whipped up from a puddle by the agile wind, smacks him in the face.

Before going back into the burrow, at the bottom of their refuge, he gropes around for his gamebag, grabs hold of the strap, and takes it with him without verifying its contents. Without being able to explain why, he's convinced the rabbit is still there. The animal hasn't escaped. He waited and fell asleep under the orange-scented dish towel.

"Any news from the front?" asks Dumestre, whose voice surprises Tristan at the cave's entrance.

Tristan wasn't expecting him to be so close. He can't see him. When he went outside, Dumestre was lying down, dozing, but now he seems to be seated. His voice is coming from higher up, it's better placed, he's articulating more clearly. Tristan senses danger, as if his companion were preparing to spring on him, but to what end? What reason would he have to harm Tristan? They're stuck with each other.

Tristan doesn't answer Dumestre's question. He doesn't tell him about the hurricane rumbling outside. He keeps quiet. Then takes a deep breath and says, in a flat voice, leveled by fear: "You're sitting up?"

28

Breakfast with Astre. Trembling knees. Tristan can smell her scent everywhere, in the white of the bread, in the steam from the tea, her softness in the butter, her sweetness. He can smell her on his fingers, in his mouth. He doesn't dare look at Mrs. Klimt. He thinks she's angry. How does she know? And what does that mean for him? He focuses on his hostess to avoid thinking about what's making him suffer: What will his life be like afterward?

He has sunk into the pain of initiation. How can he think about anything else? How can he do anything else? Or want to do anything else? Astre has become his goal, his destination. She is both question and answer, hunger and satisfaction. She is his universe.

She's going to leave in a few minutes. She has already put on her coat. She eats everything she finds on the table. With disgust, Tristan observes her shiny chin, her thick nose, which moves strangely when she chews. She is unattractive. But she is his master, his god, the condition for his existence.

So, when she heads to the ground-floor bedroom to get her suitcase, Tristan springs up after her, glues himself to her back, slips his hand under her coat, under the belt of her pants. She turns around brutally and pushes him with all her might. He falls backward.

"Are you crazy? Maniac!" she shouts.

Mrs. Klimt hurries over.

"It's nothing," says Tristan in English, in a shaky voice. "I fell."

He gets back up and thinks, I fell.

Astre leaves.

"I hope you rot, you old tramp," she croons tenderly in French while giving Mrs. Klimt a hug.

The days that follow seem coated in mud. Light can't filter through anymore. Tristan regrets his past frivolity, the peaceful sweetness of his solitude, his anonymous wanderings through the streets of London. He can't read, nor can he concentrate in Hector's lessons. He watches women, wonders how to attain them, touch them. He carries his desire like a grail, heavy and sacred. He is the knight, the lady, and the dragon all at once. Shut away, excluded.

How do they do it? Tristan wonders. The pedestrians, the ticket inspectors, the mothers, those adults he passes in hundreds, in thousands, on the streets—those who, like him, have done it. How do they manage to cross the boulevards, accomplish their tasks, speak, listen? What is this power holding them back, chaining them to themselves, forbidding them from throwing themselves on top of one another in a permanent embrace?

That's exactly what I was saying, the rabbit mumbles in a faraway voice, as though now expressing himself from some hereafter. Your kind lives under the curse of sex. Your fall is constant. It doesn't get you anywhere, because the movement is endless. You've kept your instinct, but you've emptied it of its meaning. That's why your existences are fated to misery, your brains to foolishness, your bodies to degeneration. You're never appeased; you're never satisfied. The more time I spend near you, young man, the more I love my life. I'm full of delight with the idea of being an animal. Just the thought that I escaped the pitiful human destiny fills me with joy. Your kind is the ridiculous exception. You're born losing. Young man, you give me so much in opening up to me. You give me the desire to be me, to live and to die, whether from a bullet or the jaws of a fox, the wheel of a car or a stone thrown by a child.

In the blackness of the cave, Tristan follows his divergent paths. He has separated in two. Point and counterpoint. On one side, the faceless face-to-face with Dumestre, who's now roaming around their cramped abode, happy with his rediscovered mobility, joking, threatening, incomprehensible. On the other, the mute conversation with the rabbit, who seems to be breathing with more and more difficulty at the bottom of the gamebag.

Before the wheel fully starts to turn, before his companion reveals the nature of his scheme, which Tristan feels can only be deadly, he would like to find the way to defend his condition, to think up the arguments of an appeal for his species.

What's the point of stopping the fall? Tristan asks. What's the point of looking for a purpose if the fall itself is good? Why must we aspire to satisfaction? Your brain is too small and your heart too lazy to understand the beauty, the grandeur, the glory of the energy that motivates us and permeates us. I wouldn't trade anything for my fall. I'm intoxicated with speed, and sometimes, when the chance for a moment's respite distracts me from it, it just makes me taste my comfort more, because I know it is fleeting.

Little rabbit, you will never know victory over the absurd, something we accomplish every day, every second of our existence. What renders our exaltation superior to yours is that, contrary to you, we are desperate. I know, I understood, you've convinced me: I accept that your kind possesses a consciousness of death; I'm even ready to make myself its herald, to bring the news to my own kind. You know you're mortal, but you're saved by direction. Each of your actions is logical, useful, efficient. Let's call it the law of nature. What relief, certainly, but what boredom! I'm going to tell you what you will never have, what you must envy us for, the nugget you must bring back to your kind: what you're missing is the possibility to do anything you want, to act in spite of common sense, to wring the neck of productivity, reason, causality. We alone have the power to act against our own good, but sometimes, believe me, by heading toward our loss, we access a supreme good, a superior quality of being, a real presence more intense than anything you could ever see or feel. We are constantly fighting, against ourselves, against our instincts: we search, we wander, we make mistakes, and, thanks to these detours, these refusals, we raise ourselves up; even from within our fall, we fly, we transcend.

Yes, yes, responds the rabbit in a voice pushed with difficulty through his throat by his slowing blood. "Transcendence," a word as long as a day without wild thyme. I've heard it spoken of. It's... What do you call it? Believing in God...

Just the opposite: Believing in nothing. Believing you're finished, kaput, at your limit, and weeping in the face of the rising sun, because of its beauty. Trying to reproduce this feeling, to summarize it. Being in love.

Love? pronounces the rabbit, his voice becoming more and more ethereal.

Tristan thinks about Emma and the moment when, so long ago, they entered her garden-level apartment, drowned in gray half-light because of the storm. They were soaked, hardly knew each other, had spoken to each other only three times on the bench in Brockwell Park. For some time already, he had renounced that thing he didn't have a name for: girls, love, sex? I'm too young, he had said to himself. Too foreign, too isolated to hope for it to happen—looking at them, yes, maybe, he does that sometimes in the cafeteria at the university, where he started taking classes in September, but to slip his fingers there where it smells sweet, acidic, like the sea air, no, that will never happen to him again. He contents himself with reading books, certain books in particular, to contemplate the pictures, to be his own alpha and omega. He isn't suffering anymore. He isn't waiting anymore. It's like he's in exile, at the outskirts of the world in a place he will never leave, because he doesn't know anyone, no one knows him, he's foreign and no one taught him what to do.

But Emma spoke to him, and each time she opens her mouth, he feels curious, alert, as if he is about to make an important discovery. He doesn't look at her, doesn't dare, doesn't think about it. Her act of speaking creates a sort of veil, a wall. He hears her voice, her French voice with its blunt consonants, its evasive syllables. She says words like "bougie" for bourgeois, refers to drugs by their street names, pronounces words that none of his professors here ever uses. He doesn't understand what's happening to him and even forgets to wonder why this comforts him so much. He doesn't realize that he misses French. What importance do words have? What importance does an accent or intonation have? Did he sleep with Astre out of a love for his native tongue? Is it because Emma speaks the same language as his cousin that he takes so much pleasure in listening to her? A strange pleasure, without expectation, immediate and complete. He desires nothing more, there on the bench. On the second evening they met, he pictured himself in the same situation with Astre and it didn't work. Astre is so rude, he thought, surprising himself with this judgment. Astre is mean. She has a viper's tongue. She called my mother a slut and Mrs. Klimt an old hag. She speaks only to insult people.

"Wanna do it again?" All the same, that was something. Music, power, honey, poison. He can hear her voice all too clearly expressing the irresistible proposition. "Wanna do it again?" That was nice; that was magical. But insufficient. Emma speaking, that's another sound, no serpents, no pearls either. He searches and searches, and here's what he finds: vigor, honesty, vision. Emma speaks, and the world finds itself simplified, clarified, expanded.

And then, one day, she kisses him on the mouth, on the bench, and he tells himself that he should have done that, he could have taken that initiative. Just as soon, in this kiss, he feels that he hurt her, because he waited, because he forbade himself from thinking about it.

Everything has always failed with Emma.

Soaking wet, they enter the apartment where gray half-light reigns, and, soon, their bodies are dyed the same shade of gray, urban and stormy. They don't know how to approach each other. They bump into each other, jostle, fall, get hurt. Their hands lag behind their mouths. Is it shyness that makes their blood pump? What is this solemn thing that hurts, that takes the heart like a bear claw and crushes it?

Tristan doesn't know. He doesn't have a name for that either. With his head on Emma's chest, staring, marveling one of her plum breasts, he wonders how in the world he's going to protect her, his eyes full of tears, his jaw tightened against a sob born from his gratitude, from his fear of losing her, from the idea that one day, even a long time from now, she will die.

That's just what I was saying, grumbles the rabbit, exasperated. You separate. You split up. You think you're superior for this reason, but you're only fooling yourselves. I feel so much tenderness for you, young man, but I'm ashamed when I listen to you. I'm ashamed of the fragmented existence you lead. Absence of continuity. Sterilizing classification. Categorizing is murder. This woman, Emma, if everything has failed with her, leave her. And don't tell me about love. As if I don't know what it is. Your awkward passion, your distance, the respect she inspires in you. Bullshit.

You don't understand, Tristan responds, his hand on the animal's neck. I've found what separates us, you and me. Your kind and mine. You're aware of your own finiteness, I accept that, I can agree, but you're completely unaware of the finiteness of others. That's where love is born.

29

How did this happen? How long has it taken? Why couldn't they get away? How is it that they're now swimming against the current of a slow-flowing river of mud? Can their feet touch the ground, even only from time to time? No.

Farnèse and Peretti, in the night, reach out their arms bogged down with mud, their legs hindered by their soaked pants. They kick their feet, let themselves float a little, then start again. If someone were to ask them where they're going, they wouldn't know how to respond; they'd keep quiet, frightened as they are by the necessity forcing them to thrash about in this way, as best they can, entirely spent, in order to reach a point they can't even see and wouldn't know how to locate any more than they'd know what to call it.

Sometimes, the darkness lights up: a flash, a hole in the clouds and the moon shining like the sun, outlining frightening shadows, like an eclipse at midday.

"There, to the right," Peretti murmurs. "See it?"

"What?"

"On the roof. Isn't that where the kid lives?"

"Tristan?"

"Yeah, the kid. Isn't that his house over there?"

Peretti hesitates to extend his finger and point to the exact place, fearing he'll drown if he relaxes his efforts.

Farnèse breathes in, breathes out, speeds up.

"Someone's on the roof. Look!"

"I see," Farnèse answers without turning around. "That's her, that's his wife."

"You know her?"

"Not really, but I know that's where they live. I know that's her. Smart of her to climb up on the roof. Do you know about her and Dumestre?"

"Her and Dumestre?" Peretti asks while swallowing a mouthful of mud that he spits back out, half coughing.

"Don't die," says Farnèse.

Peretti panics, speeds up, takes another gulp. "Shit, help me!"

Farnèse grabs on to a branch. He feels around underneath him, manages to find his footing, reaches a hand out to Peretti. They stay like this for a few moments, docked at the top of a tree, regaining their breath.

"Maybe it's over," says Farnèse. "I don't know. They were quiet about it."

"How'd you know? Shit, how'd you know?"

"What's it matter?"

"And you left them there? The two of them? Dumestre and the kid? In the forest? Even though you knew?"

"Yeah."

"You did it on purpose?"

"Yeah."

"Why?"

Farnèse lets go of the branch. He goes back to swimming as quickly as possible toward the objective whose nature still eludes him.

"Why?" repeats Peretti, splashing along after him.

Farnèse doesn't reply. The explanation would take up too much time, too much space. It would likely take over everything: his head, the air, the sky. He knows how to turn into an urn. He's already done it. An urn of grief, filled with liquor, wine, *eau de vie*.

He can't explain it, but a connection exists between Vladimir's death and this story. "Vladimir's death"—he never thinks about it in those words. Normally, he just thinks "Vladimir," and the name takes up all the space, swollen with tenderness, anger, regret. Someone has to take revenge, he thinks, a thought at once hazy and clairvoyant, the sort of thought produced by alcohol. Someone has to pay. There is an urgent need for justice to be rendered. In the past, people killed each other, killed themselves, for less. In books—the books he used to read—it meant gloves thrown to the ground, meetings at dawn, bring your witnesses: tales of duels with pistols, with swords. Suicide was also a type of duel, between self and self. He should have thought about it, should have followed through. He hasn't done it. He told himself he should live on as a witness to the child's past presence, a child for whom he might be the only one to grieve. But that's not true. He hasn't done it and there's no good reason for that, even the hope of redemption.

The kid's wife. Shit. A woman like that. When they showed up in the village, he recognized her right away. That type of woman. There was a lot of talk about them at first. They didn't have jobs. In any case, they never went out at normal times. Sometimes people saw them at the supermarket, the gas station. They lived in a shabby house, but they still had some means with which to do the shopping. What could it be? At least if they had a child, people would've known, from the school, on the record, under "Parents' Occupations." Farnèse was friends with the youngest teacher there, Nino's mom. She would've told him. Just friends? he wonders. But it's a rhetorical question. He knows the teacher's in love with him, has been for quite a while, not just since her husband left her. Women like her fall for him. Women like that. The kid's wife. Her too. She should have fallen for him. It would have been better for everyone. Because he never tries anything with women, he hardly looks at them or listens to them, doesn't touch them. He would've become her confidant. But she chose Dumestre. He doesn't understand. Would've loved not to know. But he saw them. Would've rather surprised them in a fit of bestiality. He spied them, without wanting to, in a tender moment—he shouldn't have been there—in midconversation after making love. Naked bodies, her sitting, him lying down, both smiling. Speaking in low voices, with secrecy. Laughing. Stroking each other's cheeks. Farnèse gazed at her body. It had been a long time since he had really seen a woman's skin. This one is special, he thought, trying to understand what distinguished her from the others, the others he couldn't see. This one doesn't have any marks or traces. As if she has never worn clothing. She was sitting in the clearing like a cow, a goose. The placidity of her body fascinated him. He was sure

Dumestre didn't notice it. What a waste. Then Dumestre lifted his hand toward her breast—not white, not brown, a breast as innocent as a forehead—and kneaded it distractedly. She smiled, a hint of contempt on the corners of her lips. Death, thought Farnèse. They must be put to death. The kid must kill them. Kill the fat one, kill the pretty one, kill them both. Farnèse doesn't know why this gave him relief, as if the reparation of this injustice had the power to compensate for all the others. Rigor. Bravery. Honor. And if there are casualties, if he kills him, if he kills her, I'll stop drinking. I'll start over.

Peretti starts shouting.

"Dammit, wait for me! I'm gonna drown."

"No," says Farnèse, whose voice is covered by the rain, the wind, the roaring water.

"Help, I'm drowning!"

Farnèse turns around, amused by the involuntary theatricality of these words. He watches as Peretti starts to drown. He hesitates. A slowness, weighed down by the full extent of his sadness suddenly being deployed, as if the urn that has been sealed for years were finally being poured out, holding his body back. He sees Peretti's head disappear, then reappear, watches his arms beat at the waves around him as though observing the whirling flight of a moth. Then he makes a decision, abruptly and quickly, like a stone launched by a slingshot, propelled by his former agility. He grabs Peretti under the arms, hoists his companion up onto his back, half drowning himself, but without fearing it. He swims, his eyes looking for some kind of support, some refuge, glimpses part of a wall, some rocks emerging from the water. It's the Gallo-Roman tower. If it's held up until now, it'll hold on one more night. He swims up to it, puts down his burden, makes sure he's breathing, he's stable, pats him on the back, explains that he has to go, there's no more danger, the water won't rise much more, he must wait there without moving, you better not move, but I've gotta go back, I have to go. Like a stone launched by a slingshot, he rushes into the current, which he catches up with and conquers. He's forgotten the fatigue. He doesn't need to try anymore.

30

With her knees against her chest, her big eyes open and incredulous, Emma sits huddled up at the top of her roof. She had climbed the attic stairs, hoisted herself up onto the beams, removed the shingles in the weakest place, balanced a stool on a table, and, for a brief moment, thought: I could hang myself.

The apparatus was perfect, easily identifiable, as readable as a pictogram: beam, stool, table. The only thing missing was the rope, but a rope was nothing.

Hang myself, yes, quite easily, to end that which I have no other way of ending. Hang myself to punish myself (with these words, blood rushes to her stomach, her head, the trance of relief, the waltz of vanquished guilt), mmm, how good it would feel to be a good girl. But it wouldn't last. The punishment wouldn't know how to wash away insults or make stains disappear. Emma would like to be less grandiose, more honest, surrender more openly to remorse; she can't manage it. In spite of everything, in spite of her shame and her disgust with herself, she holds on to a certain resilience, a vivacity that frightens her.

After all, wouldn't it be just as easy to not climb up, to let the water rise, trap her, engulf her? She pictures her self-portrait: Lady Macbeth tinted with Ophelia. It's right. It's perfect. The joy her brain brings her is limitless. Lady Macbeth and Ophelia in the same body, the wife and the virgin, the criminal and the suicidal, the Machiavellian and the wide-eyed girl.

She's going to save herself. Save her skin to save her head. She knows it's not necessary to take refuge on the roof. The water has risen only a few feet inside the house. But how can she resist the image: woman crouching on the rooftop, vigilant crow, heroine. Her desire to live is such that she prefers to take all precautions, at the risk of adopting the most grotesque poses, of making a show of it.

And Tristan?

Tristan has to start by changing his name to something less *triste*. He should be called Glad.

Why am I so cheerful? Emma wonders. Why am I so stupid?

It's because of the storm. Storms are entertaining, with the lightning, the thunder, all this water falling, the river going crazy, the power lines crashing down, the mud getting everywhere, the cars floating like toys, the black night like the heart of a forest, the explosions, the water adopting the sky's usual texture—it will never stop.

I've always suffered from delusions of grandeur, Emma says to herself. In Noah's time, God triggered the catastrophe to punish all of humanity; today, he's taking the trouble to chastise me, no one but me, a small, unique specimen. Granted, the storm is only local, but still. There will be flooding, injuries, maybe even drownings.

The elation suddenly ends. Pain replaces it. Sorrow.

Emma starts to cry. For a second, the rain ceases, the wind calms down. The tears burn her face. She shudders. From afar—but how can she hear anything coming from that far away, and in spite of the roaring waters?—she perceives the screams of a tiny child.

31

Farnèse, the Tightrope Walker, splits the water, as light as a *Gerris*, that skating insect who skims across the surface of rivers. He recovers his lost agility, revived by weightlessness. He likes being alone on the rooftops, as before, closer to the sky than the earth, invigorated by the atmosphere, alone to look at the world from on high. But tonight, high and low merge, and for him, losing the ground below means compensation, reconciliation. He has never wanted to tread on the earth, to leave the slightest footprint; he's always been up high, until the fall. Stop thinking about it. He glides ahead, getting closer, using his feet to push away alder branches as if they were tall grass. Alder trees from the banks of the river, their trunks bathed in mud, their branches tickling and scratching his ankles. He keeps along the riverbed, having found the route once more. The church is on the right, dark and severe, deprived of the smile that appears each night from the incandescent spotlights arranged at the foot of the steeple. They've all blown out. Not one light is left. The church has gone back to the dismal outfit it wore the evening it was built. Then city hall goes by, a stucco cube with pretty letters, bloodred on a meringue pediment. Then come the school and the houses, then nothing more, the alders again, poplars, ash trees, and, beyond that—yes, it's definitely coming from here. Bursting from this black hole, blacker than the metallic night, is the cry he's been hearing.

A house with a skylight at the point of its gable, far away from everything, isolated; the house at the water's edge, the old windmill.

Is it possible to be swept along even faster when the wind picks up and agitates the waves, mixed with leaves and debris? Farnèse leaps from one crest to another, his face whipped by twigs, leaves, thorns. He is joyful, without memory. Sometimes, a shape appears out of the dark, narrow frame he has chosen to reach: a white oval, a mauve wing like a turtledove's. It's a face, it's a hand, a hand reaching out. Farnèse seizes it, projected toward the face whose eyes, black pebbles emptied with fear, stare at him.

"Take him. Take the baby. I brought him up here, but if I keep him, I'm going to die. I'm going to drown. Help me. Drown the baby. I won't say it was you. I can't do it. I tried. But I've been taking care of him for three months. I know him. He depends on me. For you, it's nothing. I'll give him to you and you can leave him in the water. I don't want to die. Drown him. For you, it's nothing. He won't realize it. He'll think he's going to sleep."

The mauve hand, the turtledove wing, holds a package out to Farnèse. Farnèse recognizes the cry. This is the cry he swam for.

"Don't tell anyone what I told you. It's our secret. I won't say anything either. It'll be the river's fault. Can you? Is that okay?"

Farnèse takes the package, holds it above the water.

"Get out of here," he orders. "Go in the direction of the current, let it carry you, don't fight it, float if you can; don't hold on to any branches, just use your arms to avoid obstacles, don't try to stop yourself. The faster you go, the faster you'll be rescued. You're going to make it. I won't say anything. We never saw each other. Do what I told you."

She disappears.

Farnèse doesn't take the time to watch her float away; he looks over to his right. The child is crying very softly; he is light in Farnèse's palms, which lift up the child like a baptism.

The sycamore tree with round stumps, the one where the walking path starts at the side of the hill—is it still standing? Farnèse squints, raindrops pecking at his eyeballs, crows' beaks at a gallows feast. He grasps the package with one hand while paddling with the other; he recognizes the flaky gray and whitish spots of the tree's bark shining there, just a little farther.

Sometimes the child slips under the water. Farrnèse doesn't know if he's dead or alive—he's not making any more noise—but dead or alive, Farnèse has to save him, so he keeps going. He clutches a fistful of leaves that rips off immediately, is plunged downward, comes back up, catches hold of a branch, climbs up, pulls himself out of the water, the mud, jumps from branch to branch, sees that the waters are still rising, continues his ascent. Now he's rising into the jumble of leaves that the rain can hardly penetrate.

A strange heat sheltered in the treetops, a refuge.

He sits on a branch, contemplates the water below, a few yards under him, examines his parcel: calm pearl face. Farnèse thinks he sees a nostril quiver. He doesn't have the courage to know any more. Quickly, he unties the scarf around his neck and uses it to fasten the swaddled body to the largest branch he can find. He makes sure it will hold up, withstand the storm, won't fall, fly away, get carried off, and he dives. Leaves, leaves, branches, leaves, branches and branches and branches, leaves, branches, mud.

32

Is the earth collapsing? Did he not reinforce the walls enough? Have his instincts deceived him?

A weight comes crashing down on Tristan's back. In the darkness of the cave, a warm, compact mass cuts off his breath, crushes his ribs. He struggles, tries to breathe, turns over, throws a punch, his fist sinking into a sticky, flexible material. His legs come to his rescue. His heels stomp, strike the ground, helping to brace his torso. He frees himself, punches at the air, feels around, crawls away, escapes.

Immediately, the mass crashes down on him once more. It flattens him. It's an animal, a bear, a monster. It's trying to kill him. That's what he tells himself. Something's trying to kill me. He rolls over, gets hit in the jaw, hears a joint crack. How can he defend himself without being able to see anything? What good is it to throw blind punches? He receives a few of them, in the head, the stomach, the groin. He's being attacked; he's being stoned. He goes down to the ground. He's being crushed. He loses his breath, no longer knows when to breathe in, when to breathe out. He gasps for air. The mass moves away. Tristan stretches out his arms, draws them back in, grips his own body, as if fighting against himself. His face is squashed against the ground. A weight on his neck. He can't breathe anymore. Starts to fade. His arms shake; his legs move around, gain their footing, send the beast flying. His lungs welcome the damp air with a cry.

"Stop!" Tristan shouts. "Stop, Dumestre!"

But how does he know it's Dumestre? It's too dark for him to understand where the attack came from.

"Dumestre," he cries. "Help me! Shit, what the hell is this?"

The mass withdraws, moves back, retreats. A laugh bursts out a few inches away.

When Tristan reaches in that direction, in search of some meaning, he's dealt a fresh punch in the shoulder.

Tristan squats down, huddles in a corner, waits, suppresses the whimper of pain rising unwillingly from his rib cage. And suddenly, he throws himself forward, to defend himself, to kill. He jumps and hits, slaps, punches, head down like a ram; he finds a throat, seizes it, feels the blood pumping under his thumbs, the knee jabbing his stomach, the animal resisting. He loves pressing the carotid artery, squeezing the esophagus, crushing the trachea. Hilarity rises in him, intoxicates him. Never has he felt so strong. Never has he had so much fun.

But abruptly, he lets go.

He thought about the rabbit at an inopportune moment, as though the animal's life were more important than his. Where is the gamebag?

Silence, panting, hiccups, coughing, wheezing.

"That's nice, huh?" a sharp, hoarse voice says very close to his face, as though lying on the same pillow.

"Fuck you, Dumestre," says Tristan while groping around, searching for his bag.

This time, I'm sure I killed the rabbit, he thinks. I didn't protect him. He trusted me. He was counting on me to save him. I made him a promise. If he has survived, everything that went wrong will have been made right.

"I'm not the one who's fucked," Dumestre articulates calmly.

His voice is firm, more present, disturbingly gentle.

"The one who's fucked," he continues didactically, "is your wife."

Tristan keeps quiet. He regains his breath, touches his face, wipes the blood from his jaw with the back of his hand.

"All women are," adds Dumestre. "You don't know about it. You don't know anything. You're nothing but a rookie. You haven't pushed the shopping cart."

I want to sleep, Tristan thinks, resting his cheek on the gamebag, finally recovered. It's nothing. It's over. My rabbit is dead. Dumestre is delirious. I can't make head or tail of his story. A delirious bull. I'm going to fall asleep listening to his words, it'll be like a lullaby. And if he kills me in my sleep, I don't give a damn. I don't have the strength. I want to sleep.

"The shopping cart," Dumestre starts again. "The one you push around while your brats wait at home. You don't know they're too little to stay home alone. Did someone tell you? No, no one told you. How were you supposed to know? So there you are, like an idiot, with your cart in the grocery store and the female customers looking at you with pity. They know your wife left you. They can see it right away, thanks to your three-day-old beard, your unironed dress shirt, and then because you don't know which box to choose from the wall of cereal. They have pity on you, and they're right, because you're the cuckold, you're the ass. Meanwhile, your boys get bored at home all alone—the bitch took the TV. At first, they play with toy trains, Legos, but they're tired of that, so they decide to try something else, big-boy stuff: bathroom cleaners, kitchen gadgets, scissors, chemicals, knives, solvents, dishwasher fluid, casserole dishes, laundry detergent. They make themselves a snack, set things on fire, swallow their mixture. And you, you're still at the grocery store, pushing your cart around like an idiot. But you don't know what it's like, kid. You don't have little punks who set things on fire, blind themselves, burn themselves, and destroy your pad. Listen, I'm not complaining! My kids aren't dead. The ambulance, the firefighters, the insurance company, the police—all that was long ago. Now, they're strapping young men who are smarter than me. No one's dead. Now when I go to the grocery store, I bring my wife, the new one, but I stay in the car, in the parking lot. Never again will I touch a shopping cart.

"Your wife doesn't even do the shopping," continues Dumestre after a moment. "*Madame* is above that. *Madame* is an 'artiste.' And you, you don't care. The cart means nothing to you. Except while you're out grocery shopping, you know what I'm doing? You know what I'm doing with your wife who's so far above all that?"

Tristan dozes off. He sees pictures. Dumestre with his cart. Dumestre facing the wall of cereal. He's moved. His companion is a good storyteller. He feels the evening was a success: the little match girl, and now, the man with the shopping cart. Tristan is calm. His whole body relaxes. His lungs expand, breathe in the earth's odor, like the nape of Emma's neck beaded with sweat.

His wife. Yes. There's something wrong with his wife. Dumestre is right in the middle of explaining.

I go shopping, he recaps for himself, and during that time... During that time, Dumestre does something with my wife. My wife who is above everything.

A more violent blow, harsher than all the others, hits his spinal nerve. A blade lashes his insides. The pain is unprecedented. Yet Dumestre didn't move. Dumestre didn't touch him.

Tristan grimaces, his teeth hurt, as if he's holding back tears. He doesn't want to hear what Dumestre is saying. He wants to plug his ears, lock up his imagination. He wants to fold over on himself, flee the scene. Erase, erase, erase. Water on his face, that's what he needs. Not rain, not mud, but water from a stream, from its source, pure, untouched, to wash his hands, to splash his face.

That was Emma. Emma was the source.

Never again? he wonders. All while Dumestre explains the how, the when, the why.

He doesn't listen, but snippets of it enter his ears occasionally: A harsh, brainy woman. Not easy. Never known one like her. Why do they betray us? Though I'm definitely the one who betrayed mine, I've got nothing to blame her for. She picked up the crumbs the first one left behind.

She stuck me back together like a puzzle. I wasn't appreciative. It's awful. I felt guilty. I didn't want to keep going, but with your wife, someone else's wife, it was like we became different people, like we were new. She tossed me off anyway. Spitefully. She's a spiteful woman.

"You don't know anything about my wife," Tristan murmurs reluctantly.

And then he thinks, No one knows about my wife, because she's my wife. All that you and others see is the river, the polluted current, the raging waters, but only I know how to go back to the source, bathe in it, because she's my wife.

And, with these words, finally, he falls asleep.

33

They count. They recount. It's the only thing they know to do, except there's no more to count. Tristan and Emma don't have a penny to their names. The prefect's money transfers stopped coming one month after his protégé left the university and his room at Mrs. Klimt's.

Tristan didn't go back to Hector's. He lives at Emma's, in her arms, in her vision for the future. He is more alone than ever. Yet he's with her. The two of them are alone, and that's worse.

"Tomorrow, we're leaving," she announces to him. "We're going back to France."

"How?"

"I have a plan. Someone will bring us over on a boat. After that, we'll hitchhike. We can't stay here anymore. There's my stepmother's house. She's dead. I have the keys. We'll go there. It's in a field, in a village. Life won't cost anything. We'll plant vegetables."

"I have to say good-bye to them," says Tristan.

"To whom?"

"To Mrs. Klimt, to Hector. I have to say thank you."

"We don't have time. We have to pack. We have to leave."

"Let me go see them."

"No. They're old. They're used to it."

"They've already lost a son," argues Tristan, not sure of anything, ignorant of his host family's true history, as crumbled as his own existence.

"That's every parent's destiny," Emma responds. "All parents lose their children. You're not going to change that."

On the boat—a feminine vessel leaving the port of Dover, a masculine *navire* coming up alongside Calais—they wrap their arms around each other's waists. "Happy" isn't the right word. Ambitious, afraid, armed with orphans' courage.

"I'm going to write books," she promises him. "I'll sell thousands of 'em. We'll get through this."

"What about me?" asks Tristan.

"You?" says Emma, laughing. "You're young, you have time. You'll find something."

34

With his round black watermelon-seed eye, a turtledove contemplates his plumage. He shakes himself off, swells his vain chest. His wings are dry. Dawn, which perfectly matches the hues of his feathers, is breaking. A ray of sunlight splits the mauve band of clouds and lands on his tail. The bird shivers, takes a few meticulous steps on the sycamore branch, then lifts off, remaining motionless above the tree for an instant, carried by an upward current.

Suspended in the air, the turtledove observes the valley. The colors have changed, along with the substance. It looks like someone peeled away the earth, like the ground molted. It's ugly. The turtledove perches on a branch again, sinks into the leaves, plants his fine talons into the supple bark mottled in brown, gray, and cream. He spots a big nest a little lower in the tree, hops down to reach it. A package, poorly tied, shoddy architecture, no twigs, no artistry. What bird could have made this?

He gets closer, pecks, prodding with his beak and feet. But suddenly, the package stirs. There's something soft inside—what could this be? Is it a cocoon? What type of larva would dare stick itself to his tree like this? Something fidgets and bawls. A dreadful sound gushes out. The turtledove, seized with fear, wildly flaps his wings, gets tangled in the leaves, fails his takeoff, tries three more times, and bursts forth all at once from the green jumble into the thoroughly rinsed blue sky.

Down below, a fireman—busy clearing up the rubble, probing holes and piles of fallen rocks for survivors—hears the baby.

At first, he doesn't understand where the crying is coming from. He looks up, doesn't see anything. Thinks for a moment about storks, and the legend in which babies are dropped off at their homes by those trusty birds with long beaks. He rushes in the direction of the sound. He has been combing the ground since five this morning; he found three bodies, three corpses. It's his first emergency. He signed up as a volunteer to impress the ladies. He's been telling himself that by the time the Bastille Day ball comes around, he'll be raking them in. He doesn't have confidence in his face, because his nose is too long and always a little red because of his badly spaced teeth, but thanks to his training, he's starting to take pride in his body. With the uniform's prestige on top of that, the girls will drop like flies. His name is Jean, but everyone calls him Jean-Jean, which doesn't help with the ladies either. Before today, he had never seen a dead person. Not in real life. He is nineteen years old.

Jean-Jean runs, reaches the sycamore, looks up, listens carefully. It's coming from up there. The smooth trunk doesn't offer any grip. The mud that coated it during the night and the water it soaked up have made the bark slippery. The child keeps crying. It's an emergency, Jean-Jean repeats to himself, stamping from one foot to the other, powerless. What do you do in case of emergency? What has he already learned in training? The captain talked all day. You had to take notes, like at school. Jean-Jean never liked school. While the captain was speaking, he was admiring the deformed reflections in the nickel helmet, neither gold nor silver in color, a metal as smooth as water. Call your team, but how? He's the only one in this area. There's so much to do. They were ordered to not split up. They didn't listen. They wanted to be heroes, every man for himself. The best thing would be to save a girl, a girl whose clothes had all been ripped off by the storm, and who he, Jean-Jean, would carry, naked, in his arms, without looking at her, with total respect, and the girl would let her head fall on his chest, feel his swollen biceps, say to him: You rescued me, and afterward, they wouldn't necessarily get married, but hey, it would be a good start.

The baby cries louder and louder. What an irritating sound. How do parents do it? Jean-Jean wants it to stop. He has to find him. He must find him.

He touches the rope wound around his chest. If he doesn't mess this up too much, if he can manage to throw the rope around the lowest branch, he'll be able to hoist himself up. He imitates the movement cowboys make with their lassos, but that doesn't do anything, the hemp snake falls down on his head, so he tries whatever he can think of, jumps, throws, jumps again. From afar, it looks like he's dancing, like Pan in a fireman's costume.

It works, the rope goes over. He makes a slipknot, grabs on, and lifts himself up, legs at right angles, abs on fire. He'd love for someone to see him now.

Once he's up in the leaves, he regains his boyhood reflexes. He leaps and launches himself from one branch to another, and suddenly, he's there in front of the package, tied up in a silk scarf with a green-and-pink pattern.

Very gently, he loosens the knot, constantly afraid of dropping the wiggling, screaming baby with his toothless mouth—a furious scarlet hole. The young fireman's hands are shaking, but his thighs squeeze the branch firmly. He grabs the baby and presses him to his chest. Immediately, the crying stops, but like a spreading wave of contagion coming in contact with Jean-Jean's chest, it causes him to sob in turn, without understanding why. This time, he's happy no one can see him.

35

"A firefighter found him."

"Where?"

"Hanging in the sycamore where the walking path starts."

"How'd he climb up there?"

"Someone tied him up there."

"Who, the firefighter?"

"No, the baby. Someone had tied him up in the tree, and the firefighter found him."

"And the nanny?"

"She's in the hospital. She says she doesn't remember anything. She's in shock."

"Maybe she tied Nino up there."

"Who's Nino?"

"The teacher's son of course, the miracle baby!"

"No, that's impossible. The nanny wouldn't have been able to climb that high. I hear it was fifty feet off the ground."

"How's he doing now?"

"The baby?"

"Yes, Nino, how's he doing?"

"Fine. He was dehydrated and got quite a chill—"

"Hypothermia!"

"Yes, that's it, hypothermia. But he'll recover in no time. A good bottle, a warm bath, and he'll be as good as new! Those little guys are really tough."

"And his mom?"

"What do you think? His mom is happy, of course! Shh, be quiet, there she is."

The teacher walks forward with Nino in her arms. The whole village has come to the memorial service for the dead and missing. Some are sad, others are relieved. The young priest put on cologne to muster his courage. He's afraid that people won't appreciate the service and say it's his fault.

The teacher comes forward and everyone watches her. She is beautiful. She is full of love. She's overflowing with it. The people in the church don't know that what they're seeing, what they're admiring, is just that: overflowing love. They just think that the green-and-pink-patterned scarf around her neck brings out her eyes marvelously.

36

When Tristan wakes up, the cave is empty. He stretches.

I hurt everywhere, he realizes. The fight was abandoned, the enemy brought down—or, at least, kept at bay. But what enemy?

His clothes, moist and smelly, are scattered around him.

He feels breathless, like after a nightmare.

But that wasn't a dream, he thinks. I really did go through all that.

He slips on his clothing in the dark, diluted by the whiteness of the dawning day, and crawls out of the cave, along the tunnel to the burrow's entrance.

Standing up on his mound, he gazes at the sky's puerile outburst, the chubbiness of the hills. A naive, cleansed panorama.

He starts walking with his hand on the gamebag and feels the dead rabbit under his fingers, distractedly stroking the inert backbone through the fabric. He thinks of the night's disaster, of the headache he has, of his odor. Returning from the hunt. What fresh glory now decorates his brow?

He tries to recover his anger, to hatch a mutiny against his fate, doesn't manage, gives up from fatigue.

All the same, he continues on eagerly, happy to be alive, tasting the paradoxical mirth that comes in leaving a cemetery. At certain moments, going downhill, he starts to run, restless.

At the top of the final hill, he comes to a standstill. The village stretches out before his eyes. What's left of it. The image in front of him doesn't correspond with anything, not one emotion, not one word. It's like trying to capture a dead person's gaze. He spreads his arms open, lets them fall to his sides. His shoes are suddenly filled with lead. He can hardly lift his feet. There's no noise. No light in the windows.

The colors have changed, Tristan says to himself. It's because the contrast isn't the same; the depth is uniform, confused by the destruction. The sounds are different too, muted by the mud, swallowed up by puddles. And my odor, thinks Tristan, my odor is nothing compared with the stench stinking up the air. The sewers have been upturned like a spilled drink.

He keeps walking, bites his lips, tears the skin from the cracks, bleeds, sucks on the blood. With each new bend, with each new road, he finds piles of fallen rocks, burial mounds made of shingles, embankments of mud mixed with rubble. A car door stands up in a hedge, resembling a bird's wing. Bundles of straw wait at a broken traffic light. A clothesline adorned with corkscrewed laundry crawls laboriously along a side street, like a giant caterpillar caught in a trap. Shoes crown fallen utility poles.

When he nears the center of the village, Tristan is forced to retrace his steps—the water comes halfway up his thighs. He'll have to go all the way past the sawmill to get around the marketplace. He hurts. The pain is all over his body, high, low, outside, inside; his skin, his organs, everything hurts. The pain is also in what he sees: the torn-off shutters, the twisted drain pipes. He admires the storm's tenacity, its meticulous destruction of everything, turning everything upside down. The ironic precision with which the wind and the floodwaters have created a new landscape: here, a vacuum hanging from a bakery sign; there, an overturned table with three tires of different sizes on one of its legs, stacked on top of one another like an abacus.

Without thinking, he caresses the gamebag. He'd like to reassure the rabbit, tell him about the sun rising from behind the hill, the new day that's dawning, the relief.

He wants to go home. He wants to see his house. But how could their poor little shack have possibly withstood the storm? You never know, he thinks to give himself the strength to go even faster. He stops to peek inside a few of the buildings that were spared more than others. Voices reach him. There are survivors. It's dawn. That's why it's silent, because it's dawn. People are still sleeping. They're alive, but sleeping.

I'm lucky, he says to himself. Very lucky. I always have been. My life up to now has been easy and gentle. Joys have bombarded me, one after the other.

Tristan regains his energy. He lengthens his stride, starts running, catches sight of the sawmill, takes a short-cut, clears fences, gates; he jumps, falls, gets up, starts running again. The house is at the end of the path, in the middle of a cow pasture, protected by thistles.

The roof is gone. Decapitated, it stands, a pitiful hollow cube, over a century old. An incredulous sense of hilarity wrings his stomach. Terror seizes him. "Terror," the word that came to his mind the day his mother died, midsentence, sitting on her bed. She had said, "You're gonna laugh, but..." And nothing more. Her breathing had stopped.

Tristan calls out. He doesn't hear anyone calling back, but he keeps calling, running, breathless.

Then Emma comes out, wrapped in a winter coat, her bare legs stained with mud. She comes toward him, sinks into the earth up to her mid-calves, staggers, straightens up. He watches her come toward him, in their battered garden, in the sludge of an earth that drank too much. She halts a few yards away. Smiles at him. Her right eyebrow is scored with two red lines, her left cheek with a thin gash, beaded with drops of blood. She still has the head of an Indian chief, the eyes of pure water at its source, the look that he alone knows and recognizes.

Slowly, like a magician, he opens his gamebag to take out his surprise.

The rabbit.

He grabs the animal by the ears and brandishes him at arm's length, sticks out his chest, and presents him to his wife. I'm back from the hunt, he thinks. And, for an instant, he feels a trapper's pride.

But the ball of fur, as though animated by a spring, flails about and flies down to the ground, skates over the puddles. Only his white tail punctuates the zigzag of his flight every second or so.

Emma doesn't understand. She didn't have time to see. She stares, wide-eyed. Looks at Tristan. Looks at the white point moving away.

What is this thing dashing away, escaping from us and taking off? she wonders.

Let's just say it's your childhood, says the rabbit, before disappearing.

Translator's Note

A voice rises from a blank space, its identity enigmatic and captivating. As words stream together, you are pulled deeper into its longing, its earnestness, its desperation, all the while wondering if you will ever really know just who it belongs to…

As a literary translator, I choose works that speak to me. From this book's first words, I was so curious about the voice behind them, even after discovering that voice belonged to a rabbit with a penchant for philosophy. I was enticed, then held captive in the pages as I waited in wonder, hoping that *what went wrong would be made right* before the last sentence set me free.

Translators are readers first and foremost, and the works we choose to translate often choose us. But now I'd like to turn the metaphor on its (furry) head, because the translator must take the text captive in order to do something with it. The translator's act of choosing a text can even be considered an act of violence, a cleaner shot than

Tristan's with a far more purposeful aim, for the moment of choosing marks the beginning of the text's transformation. Not only the confines of the new language, but the translator's own interpretation wreak havoc on the text, forcing it into places the author might not even have imagined. And so, there is always conflict in the translation process. Moments when the text resists and will not be tamed, moments when the translator might decide to leave certain words untranslated, or completely rearrange the words in a sentence, or leave ambiguities unresolved.

Translators often use the space of the translator's note to discuss the nitty-gritty of the "problems" they faced in the text. But I'm not going to get into those here, because for me, this translation was so much more about diving in headfirst. *Whatever you do, don't think about it... Don't estimate what's left to accomplish, don't congratulate yourself for what's already been done... Go for it with your eyes closed, feeling confident, armed with nothing but your joy.* While this is not my first published translation, it was in fact the first full-length translation I completed, serving as the capstone project for my master's degree. It began tentatively, as I tried to aim at that enigmatic voice with my untrained hands. But at a certain point, I realized I had to just go for it and start digging, if only for the joy that translation renders.

What a beautiful encounter. The more time I spent with this text—translating it, revising it, workshopping it with others, musing on it as I went about my day—the more confident I felt recreating the voice and the story that so enchanted me from the beginning, turning the opening monologue into a conversation. Because translation truly is a conversation, and one that can get quite philosophical at times. What kind of diction might a rabbit use? How slangy should this dialog be? How can I emphasize this Biblical allusion? How can I avoid repeating this word in the same paragraph, since the French uses two different words? Does the way I've reworded this sentence make sense? Is this really the "right" word for this moment in the text? So much of translation is about finding your own answers to the questions the text raises throughout the process. And these answers, like the critical moment Tristan realizes what makes him so different from the rabbit, create the transformational differences that bring the translation into being.

In perhaps the most famous essay on translation, Walter Benjamin's "The Task of the Translator," Benjamin puts forth the idea that a translation of a text is its afterlife, because literary texts can only survive through translation. *I'm not dying… I'm persevering. I'm starting a new life, a surplus. I see our encounter as a miracle.* You see, it's only because translators choose to take texts into their care, carry them around for a bit, so to speak, and then set them free in a new place that we readers can fall in love with literary voices from elsewhere. Translators may well do violence to a text with the inevitable changes they incur, but they are also miracle workers, giving new life to something that otherwise might never have left its home turf.

But now, dear reader, this text has jumped out of my hands and into yours. I can't show you exactly what I was aiming at, but I hope you've found something miraculous in the voice and the story that captivated me in the first place.

Enough with the metaphors.

I would like to thank my fabulous cohort in the NYU MA in Literary Translation (French-English) program—Hannah, Margaret, Patrick, and Serene, as well as our fearless leaders, Alyson and Emmanuelle—for all their input as I was workshopping this book. Their voices are here, too.

Thank you to Ben Van Wyke, who showed me in those fascinating conversations at ALTA that absolutely anything can be a metaphor for translation, from Jacqueline du Pré to a hunting party, and who, sadly, is no longer with us.

Thank you to everyone at Unnamed Press who fell in love with Desarthe's story as much as I did and helped give it a new life.

And thank you to my dear husband Jonathan, for his depths of love.

—Christiana Hills

About Christiana Hills

Christiana Hills translates written works from French into English, specializing in contemporary literary fiction, with a particular interest in experimental works and the Oulipo. She is most recently the translator of Michele Audin's *One Hundred Twenty One Days* and Agnès Desarthe's *Hunting Party*. She holds a PhD in Translation Studies from Binghamton University.